A Nun's Tale
My Sister the Sister

by Richard Pump

A Nun's Tale

A Nun's Tale: My Sister the Sister

Cover design by Mia Wang
Editing by George Pimpton
Author Richard Pump

ISBN: 9798619986433

TANDEM
HOUSE
PUBLISHING
Stories that make you feel

Chapter 1

Robert English peered out the window of the speeding train. It was taking him home for the first time in eight years. Now at twenty-nine years old, he felt strong enough to take on the parents who had almost driven him insane. As he looked out the window, it didn't seem that the train was moving, as much as the scenery was moving passed the train.

He wondered how his brothers, James and Eric were fairing. Jimmy had been married the year before Robert had left. Eric, however, who was only sixteen at the time, had remained at home while Robert opted to escape and go west. He had always felt guilty about leaving them, especially Eric. The train trip turned out to be a long and tedious one with a long layover in Chicago. He probably should have flown, but his fear of flying wouldn't let him. Actually, Robert wasn't afraid of flying; as much as he was afraid of crashing.

It was now October 17th, and September 11th was just two months ago. Who knows what those Muslim screwballs had planned now. Them and their seventy-two virgins. A lot of good the virgins would do the idiots, when they are dead.

Well it wouldn't be long now. The conductor had just announced they would be pulling into Cincinnati in fifteen minutes. He wondered if anyone would be at the station. If they weren't, he would take a cab. Robert grabbed his two suitcases and moved through the train car toward the exit.

As the train pulled into the station Robert saw his brother Eric standing on the platform. He was pleased he hadn't forgotten him. Eric was easy to spot, as he towered over everyone else by at least three inches and was wearing a very tight fire engine red t-shirt that accentuated his massive physique.

Climbing down the stairs, he waived at his brother and yelled,

"Eric ... Over here."

With a quick stride, Eric ran to his brother and threw his arms around him.

"I'm so glad you are home Bob; Mom has been nuts for a week worrying that you might not show up."

"Yah ... I'm here. God Eric you look great. You been working out?"

"Everyday! I can bench my own weight now; 215 lbs. Maybe we can get to the gym before you leave."

"That would be great. How are Jimmy and Dad?"

"Jimmy and Erin are in the middle of a divorce, and Dad? Well you know Dad. He doesn't change much. The only thing he talks about is the weather, Mom's crummy meatloaf and the Bengals. If he didn't have his football every year, there would be no living with him."

"What about you kid? What's going on besides the gym?" asked Robert as Eric pushed Robert's suitcases into the backseat of his Volkswagen Bug.

"Well do you remember Darla? Darla Peek?"

"Yes, of course. I used to call her "Peek a boo". She really hated that," Robert laughed.

"I took her to the senior prom. We danced and made out on the floor of the Boy's Gym, until the teachers raised hell. They said that we were dancing too close. I can't understand what the problem was; we were both adults. Who knows, maybe they were right. Darla was rubbing her crotch on my leg, and I was rock hard. It's difficult to dance like that, yah know?"

"I know exactly what you mean. I've been there once or twice myself. So what happened?"

"Darla laid her head in my chest in the middle of a slow dance to "Earth Angel"; and whispered, 'Eric I want you to fuck me until I can't walk anymore."

"You're kidding me. Little "peek a boo" your tomboy buddy, you have known since elementary school?"

"Yah, but she ain't no tomboy no more."

"Double negative Eric; maybe triple. How the hell did you ever graduate high school?"

"Football! They couldn't keep me, 'cus one of the coaches, Mr. Dantonio wanted me to play for the "Bearcats".

"You're at the University of Cincinnati?"

"Yah, but Dad won't be happy until I'm playing for the Bengals."

"Face it kid; Dad will never really be happy!"

"I guess. So I was at the dance with Darla. She has the sweetest ass I have ever seen. Well she was humping my leg again and two of the Lesbo girl's gym teachers ordered us out of the dance. Like I gave a shit. We got in the car and drove around town looking for a motel, but it was graduation night and everywhere we went, all we saw was No Vacancy signs.

Darla was as hot as a summer in Panama and really wanted to fuck, so we went to Miller's creek, and parked under a grove of trees with the rest of the kids who couldn't get a room. Darla got out of the car and pulled her panties off. I sat where you are sitting and she got back in and sat on my lap, looking down at me smiling. Bro she has such a tight pussy."

Robert squirmed a little, knowing his brother and peek-a-boo, were fucking where he was now sitting.

"I slid my cock into her tight little quim, grabbed her bare ass with both hands and fucked her for two hours. She must have cum six or eight times, all over the pants of my rented tux. Man, the people at the tux shop were pissed and started cussing me out in Chinese. I gave them an extra ten bucks for the stains. It was worth it. I told the guy at the tux shop that he should at least give the pants a whiff, 'cause Darla's pussy smell was all over them. She has the best cunt smell ever."

"You not come back no more." the Chinese guy told me.

Robert couldn't help but laugh at his little brother's adventures on prom night. He was rough, but he had a way of telling a story that made you sit up and listen.

"So? Are you and Darla still dating, if you can call it that?"

"Naw! We went out for about three months after that. She almost wore my pecker off. She is a great fuck. But she joined the NAVY right after 911. She said she wanted to help fight the war on terrorism. I don't see it, 'cause there ain't no fuckin' A-rabs out in the ocean. She's kind of a dipsy bitch, but a really great fuck."

Eric's car turned down Lark Avenue, and all of Robert's childhood memories came flooding back into his head. Like the time he crashed his bicycle into the ice cream truck, trying to get the guy to stop. He recalled falling out of old lady Henshaw's apple tree and breaking his arm.

Then there was the time Jennifer Conley, the girl who lived next door, let him feel her up in the orchard behind her house. She came all over his hand then she sat him down and jacked him off. They dated her last year of High School, and another year before she went off to college. Whenever he couldn't get the car, they had great sex in the orchard, sometimes as much as four or five nights a week.

They both cared a lot for each other and talked about marriage, but her parents sent her away to a girl's college in Texas of all places. Robert believed that they did it just to get her away from him. What a fantastic girl he thought. She was his first love, and they got each other's cherry. He wondered if she was still single. Probably not more likely she's got six kids by now.

Eric grabbed Robert's bags and carried them up to the old house. It hadn't changed much. Maybe a new coat of paint, or maybe the old paint had just faded. They walked in the front door and Eric yelled out,

"Hey anyone home, 'the practical son has returned'."

"That's prodigal son, Eric, not practical."

"Whatever, you're home Bro."

Their Dad was sitting on the other side of the room with his back to them, and when Eric called to him, his Dad just raised a hand and said,

"Wait a minute that black kid, is going for a touchdown. Oh fuck, they got him. Ok Bengals first down. Let's go!"

Their Mom came running out of the kitchen, as much as she could at a hundred an eighty pounds and threw her arms around Robert.

"My baby. Oh, Robert I missed you so much. I made your favorite meatloaf for dinner. Mashed potatoes, gravy and string beans; the French cut type you like so much."

"You gotta eat the meatloaf Robert," said his Dad still not turning his attention away from the football game. "We don't need no more fuckin' door stops."

Robert and Eric just looked at each other. Robert wondered if there was a set length of time, he should allow his mother to squeeze the crap out of him? Maybe one minute for each year he had been gone? Shit that was eight minutes. He would be dead by then.

"Mom", Robert said in defense, attempting to get his mother's thoughts onto something else. "Do you have anything to drink; water or maybe a soda?"

"We only drink beer in this house. Give him a beer Marge." said his Father.

His mother broke her grasp on Robert, as if a phantom referee had called holding in a boxing match. She again attempted to run to the kitchen, her excess weight holding her back like she was dragging Eric's VW Bug. Eric finally dropped the bags and both of the boys followed their mother.

"Glad you're back son," said his Dad, still mesmerized by the Television.

"Thanks Dad. It's good to be home ... for a while."

In the kitchen their mother poured the boys glasses of lemonade and handed it to each of them. They both sat at the kitchen table, much like they did when they were little. Robert felt his mother was going to ask how school was that day, but she didn't.

"Robert, are you dating anyone special?"

"No mom. I was dating for a time, but girls in California are ..."

" ... weird?" Ask Eric. Finishing his brother's sentience.

"Yah ... a lot of them are weird, and I guess some of them are OK, too. All the girls I have met are weird, though. At least weird to me."

"What kind of girl are you looking for Bro? Cause I know some that ..."

Eric stopped short in his description as his mother was staring at him with her disappointed look.

"Let's just say that I know some girls, and I could fix you up. How long you gonna' be here?

"A week maybe. It depends how things go."

"What things son?"

"Just ... things Mom. Just things. Besides I have to be back to work in about ten days," he lied, feeling nervous, as when he was younger his Mother could always tell when he was lying. He didn't want anyone to know he had a full month off from work.

"We'll talk later Bro."

"OK Eric ... Thanks."

Addressing the two boys again as though they were in the forth grade she said,

"Dinner is almost ready. Go wash up boys."

Robert and Eric looked at each other smiled and shook their heads, then walked into the front room. Their dad was still in his "Lazyboy" recliner yelling at the TV.

"You fucking idiots. You couldn't win a game with a High School team. Just look at those assholes. What a bunch of jerks. They should have their salaries cut ... OK ... that's more like it. That little black fucker is gonna' get a touchdown. Good work guys."

"Dad ..." said Robert, "You are an enigma."

"Not me son, it's those fucking Bengals."

"What's an ignigma?"

"Not ignigma Eric. It's an e-nig-ma."

"What's that?"

"An enigma is, something or someone that is puzzling, ambiguous, or inexplicable."

"I know 'puzzling' Bro, but what is the other two?"

"What are the other two?"

"I asked first Bro."

"Well ambiguous is ..."

"Don't waste you're fuckin' time Robert. Eric wouldn't know a multi syllable word if it jumped up and bit him in the ass," said their Dad. "Eric is a football player, nothing else."

"Earl, leave the boys alone and quit picking on them."

"Shut up and get dinner on the table."

"If you ever looked away from the TV, you might have seen, that dinner is on the table."

"Well get me a plate; it's only the start of the fourth quarter. And get me another beer too, and not that light shit either. Get me a real beer."

Marge looked at her husband, wishing her thoughts and her nasty glances would put him out of her misery. She really hated him after thirty-five years of a loveless marriage, and she wished she hadn't wasted her life just being with the self-centered bastard. Marge then turned on her heals and went to the kitchen to get another beer for Earl.

"Dad ... Why do you talk to Mom like that? She doesn't deserve that."

"You are right son ... she deserves a good swift kick in her big fat ass; and mind your own fucking business. You weren't here when we got married, and you won't be here when we kick off."

Robert knew that he shouldn't have come home. Nothing had changed. He had only been in town for two hours and twenty-two minutes, and a new record in stupidly had already been set, he thought. Robert, Eric and their Mom sat at the table. Their Mother said grace, while their father ate, cursing the meatloaf and the football team simultaneously, burping and yelling at the TV.

I'll never make a week, thought Robert. No way in hell.

"Your meatloaf is great Mom. Just like always."

"Whad-you-do Kid, leave your taste buds in California with your brains?"

The phone rang. Earl stated that he wasn't in. Marge retorted that he never was.

"Hello? How is it going Jimmy? Is everything working out OK son? Yes Robert's here. Yes, I'll tell them son. They're eating right now. Meatloaf why? Oh ... don't say that ... you know that you always liked my meatloaf ... Ok bye ... I love you."

"Boys that was Jimmy. He would like you to call him at his apartment when you are done eating."

After that, the boys ate in silence, and except for their father, everything was fine. Dinner was over and the boys helped their mother with the dishes. She told them to call their brother Jim, as he was very lonely living by himself. Eric called and whispered to Robert, that Jim had an emergency, and he wanted them to come over ASAP.

They got in Eric's bug, and he was doing sixty-five on surface streets. When they arrived, they jumped out of the car and ran up the stairs that led to Jim's second story apartment. It was cool out and in all the haste Eric forgot his jacket. They were both concerned as they banged on the door. A calm voice answered,

"If you are Robert and Eric come on in. Everybody else fuck off."

Robert opened the door and they walked in. Robert asked,

"What was the emergency Jim?"

Jim was seated in a recliner naked except for a t-shirt, looking much like his father watching TV, except there was a triple X rated movie playing instead of football, while a girl not much over eighteen was kneeling between his legs. She had one hand lightly squeezing his balls and the other was jacking him off, while she sucked his cock.

"The emergency is, I've got three gorgeous young girls here and only one cock. You guys did bring your cocks with you? Didn't you?"

"Shit," said Eric. "I left mine at home on the dresser."

A cute little blond with wide eyes, but obviously nothing behind them, who was wearing a royal blue football jersey with a white number "5" on the front, and sexy pair of white lace panties, looked at Eric and asked,

"Really?"

"No Lisa, Eric was joking. Cocks don't come off."

"Ok! She said with a big smile ... then I'll take the one in the red t-shirt. The big guy with all the muscles," she smiled biting her lower lip, looking at Eric.

"Good," said the brunet. "I'll want the one with the sultry eyes and the sexy lips. He looks like he can fuck all night."

"OK Gina, he is all yours. He is my brother Robert."

"I don't need to know his name. How big is his cock. I need something really large to fill me up."

"Jimmy, we didn't come prepared for this. I don't have any condoms."

"It's OK Bob, the girls brought a whole bunch of them." Jim said, pointing to a brown paper bag on the coffee table. "You don't really need one for Gina if you don't want. She's on the pill."

"Where do the girls come from?"

"School. They are in my Lit class at City College. I promised all of them an "A", if they do well here tonight. He pointed to Karen, who was still sucking his cock and said,

"She already has an A plus, but she won't quit until I cum in her mouth. I don't know what to do; I can't give her a better grade than an A plus. I know what, I'll eat her pussy. That will make her happy. She really loves a good mouth fuck."

As Robert looked over at Eric, the little blond, Lisa had her panties and his t-shirt off. She was kneeling in front of him, jacking him off, mumbling,

"God look at these muscles and this cock. I won't be able to walk for days and it's only Saturday. Oh well."

The dark haired girl waked up to Robert and slowly took off his jacket, then unbuttoned his shirt. As she stared straight in his eyes, she removed his belt, and then unzipped his pants, letting them fall to the floor. She then got down on the floor and removed his shoes, and socks, rubbing her cheek against the bulge in his jockey shorts. Lifting his legs one at a time, she pulled his pants clear and tossed them in a heap.

"You won't need these for a long time." She warned pulling off his shirt.

Robert felt funny standing in the middle of his brother's apartment wearing only a pair of Jockey shorts. However, that didn't last long, as Gina pulled them down also, leaving him totally naked, his cock hard and pointing straight at her.

"If somebody didn't know you guys were brothers," said Gina, stroking Robert's cock. "They would know it after checking your peckers. Girls we have hit the "mother load". They're all good."

"Great," said Lisa her twin ponytail, blonde hair in bouncing as she sat on Eric's lap facing him on the couch, his cock disappearing into her vagina, then showing itself again.

"Mmmmmm." Said Lisa, "I like this one." Smiling she looked in his eyes and asked, "What's your name again big guy?"

"ERIC" he yelled as he came in the cute little blonde's pussy.

"Ooooo girls you're going to like him. He really fucks good. Do me harder Daddy. I like it."

Jim moaned as he began to squirt his cum in Karen's mouth. She gulped it down like it was something that had been on a menu.

Karen got up and asked,

"Which one do I get next? I need more cum in my diet. It has lots of vitamins."

"You can have this one Karen," said the blond moving over to Jim. "But take it easy, I just fucked the shit out of him."

Eric sat on the couch leaning back as though a mule had kicked him. Karen got between his legs and lifted his rather large cock. She licked it for a few minutes and then sucked on its head.

"You know Lisa," said Karen. "You don't taste bad at all. If it ever happens that we can't get some guys, you can count on me to go down on you."

"Thanks babe, me too."

Robert had Gina bent over an ottoman, holding her hips tight, shoving his cock in her cunt as hard as he could.

"Fuck my ass baby," said Gina. "Stick that thing in momma's asshole. Come on baby fuck momma. I really need it hard. Shove it in my ass. Fuck my ass."

Robert was glad he had worn a condom. When he pulled his cock from her vagina, he eased it into her butt and slowly began to fuck her rectum.

"I told you to fuck my ass hard. I'm not a beginner; I'm eighteen. Do it harder. I can take it. Shove it in me. Make me cum guy."

"Robert ... my name is Robert."

"Whatever ... just fuck me harder."

That was the first time Robert had pure recreational sex; if you could call it pure. No emotions to drag you down. Although he had never been with a whore, he imagined that it wouldn't be much different. The girls weren't really whores; but actually, when you thought about it they were. They were just fucking for grades and not for money.

Robert felt like he and his brothers were pieces of meat. He felt dejected, probably like a woman felt when her pussy was used as an available sperm dump. He took an oath as he began to cum in Gina's butt, that he would never again treat a woman like, just a piece of ass. If he didn't really care for the girl emotionally, he wouldn't fuck her. Robert was twenty-nine and finally becoming an adult. It was about time he thought.

"Jesus Christ," said Gina. "That was great. Your cock really filled up my butt guy."

Robert knew that these girls would always refer to him and his brothers as those three brothers with the big cocks. Gina had moved on to Eric, who had just been sucked off by Jim's girl, Karen. Gina began to play with Eric's cock attempting to bring some life back into it. Karen went back to Jim and stroked his cock. She said,

"You know girls. Three guys just aren't enough for us. We should have at least ten guys at a time, so somebody always has a hard on."

Robert was on his back, on the floor almost unconscious, when the little blond stripped off his condom and dropped it in a pile on the floor. She quickly sucked the limp member into her mouth and began to do what she did best.

Robert woke up the next morning, right where he had passed out on his brother's front room floor completely naked. As he looked around, he saw that Eric and Jimmy didn't have anything on either.

"Where are the girls?" asked Eric as he awoke and looked around the room.

"They left." said Jim.

"Why?"

"Because we don't own them. They have homes."

"But," Eric said, "I was going to give them extra credit."

"Robert asked, "Don't you ever get enough Eric?"

"Enough of what?"

"Sex you dork." Said Jim, "S.E.X."

"Hell no ... Do you guys?"

"You have to understand Jim, that to Eric, 'Too much Sex' is an oxymoron.

The brothers all took showers, so their mom wouldn't detect the odor of pussy on them, and slowly got dressed. They were due back at their parent's house by eleven, for a bar-b-que.

When they got in the car, Eric moved very slow, sitting down easy. After starting the car, Eric put it in gear and pulled out of the driveway. He moaned each time he turned a corner or stepped on the brakes.

"What are you moaning about Eric?" asked Robert.

"My nuts hurt."

"Did you bump them on something?"

"Yah!"

"What?"

"The girls."

Chapter 2

"How many times did you fuck them?" asked Robert.

"All of them?"

"Yes."

"'Bout fifteen times."

"Each?" asked Robert.

"No ... all together. What do you think I am?"

"A machine?" Jim said from the back seat.

"Jesus Eric, what happened then?"

"I was told that I was very good, and a date was arranged."

"With which one?

"All of them ... next Saturday. They want to have a foursome, whatever that is."

"Can you understand why his nuts hurt Jim?"

"Maybe it's too much weight lifting Bob."

"Yah that's probably it."

They arrived at the house and walked slowly so Eric could keep up with them.

As they entered the house, their mother was laying in wait like a commando ready to strike, and then grabbed each one of them for a hug.

"Is Dad ever able to get out of that chair?" asked Robert.

"Only to pee," said his mother, smiling and a little embarrassed at what she had said. "Boys we have a guest in the backyard."

The boys went out into the backyard. Seated on the swing was Robert's ex girlfriend, Jennifer Conley. She didn't appear much older than when they were dating. If she was three years younger than Robert, which meant she was now twenty-six. Her long silky blond hair was down to the middle of her back. She was wearing a Kelly green top, which set off her striking green eyes, and she had on tight white shorts. She knew Robert had always loved her in white shorts.

"Hi Bobby," she said patting the seat next to her. "Sit down a while and talk to me."

"How is it going Jennifer? You married?"

"Kind of separated right now. What about you?"

"Married? No ... not me."

"Why not Bobby?"

"I never really got over you, I guess." He whispered.

"Well thank you Bobby, but that isn't just a line to get me back into the orchard, is it?"

"No Jennifer ... no line."

"You know that I returned from college ready to fight to the death with my parents over you and I being married, but when I got here you were gone. I wrote to you, three or four letters a week, but you never wrote back. Why Bobby?" she whispered.

"The pain of loosing you was so bad I spent almost the whole first year at the bottom of Jack Daniel's bottles. My gut hurt so much that I went to the doctor thinking I had an ulcer. Then I was on a quest to find, and fuck every girl I could get my hands on. Once I had them, that was it and I dumped them. I now believe I was trying to get back at all women for what I believed you had done to me."

"I'm so sorry Robert. I have never really forgiven my parents for the pain they caused both of us. Were any of those girls ... better than me?"

"Shit ... Are you kidding me? Of course not, Jenn. What about you?"

"Well as I said, when I came back you were gone, and nobody had heard from you in a couple of years. I sent letters to your last known address, but nothing ever came back. Where were you?"

"I think that I was lost ... and looking for myself."

"Did you find yourself Bobby?"

"I guess; here I am," He said with a flourish of his arms.

"After a while my girlfriends said they were going to hold a memorial service for you, so I could get you out of my system and move on. I was working as a night nurse at Cincinnati General and met a doctor; Richard, who seemed to be very nice ... at the time. We dated for almost two years and then he asked me to marry him. As I had no other prospects, it seemed like a good idea, so we got married. The only good thing to come out of our marriage was our two children, Bobby and Shelley. Bobby is five and Shelley is almost three."

"They sound great."

"They are the only things in this universe that keep me on track. I think that without them I would die."

Just then Robert's mother came over to them carrying a large book under her arm.

"Hello children," she said. "The bar-b-que should be ready in about a half hour. Are you hungry?"

"Maybe a little Mrs. English," said Jennifer.

"I could eat too, mom."

Robert's mother sat on a lawn chair, which bent under her weight, and said,

"I brought the boy's photo album out for everybody to see."

"Just great mom." Robert said with a scowl.

Ignoring Robert's obvious irritation, she handed the book to Jennifer and asked,

"Would you like to see Robert's baby photos? He's naked in some of them."

Jennifer took the book and said, "I would love to see Robert naked." And under voice she whispered to Robert, "again".

"Well I'll leave you two to the photos. I have to turn the meat."

"Ooooo, that sounds like fun," said Jennifer smiling looking down at her ex-boyfriend's crotch.

"What dear?" asked Robert's mother.

"Nothing Mrs. English."

"Look at this one. Robert's cute little butt, Mmmm, I could just bite it."

"You did." Said Robert.

"Oh yah ... huh? Sweet meat!"

The next page was Robert in various poses. The one that caught Jennifer's eye was Robert totally naked on his back, with his legs spread, and his penis hard as a rock.

"Wow Bobby, even then. No wonder my pussy throbbed for hours after our dates." She whispered again, "I've never met anybody that would fill your ... shoes. Never!"

"So how come the split up?" asked Robert?

Jennifer shrugged and twisted her mouth in an expression of uncertainty. "Don't know. Sometimes married people just get tired of each other; I guess."

They leafed through the book then found a photo in "the religious" section. Robert was wearing a white baptismal dress. A priest was dribbling holy water on his forehead. His mouth was open, and his eyes were closed. It looked as though he was yelling to high heaven.

"I'll bet God knew he had a new member that day."

Robert laughed and agreed. His parents had told him on several occasions that his voice rattled the church's stained-glass windows. Then he saw the top of a head of somebody standing next to the priest. Turning the page, to the next photo which was taken further back so all of the participants could be in the photo, Robert saw a little girl in the picture; about four or five years old. She had beautiful little face, big wide blue eyes and a terrified expression. She was standing behind the priest, clutching his leg tightly, and sucking on what appeared to be a plastic crucifix.

"I wonder who the little girl is? I don't remember her as being part of our family."

"Maybe she's a cousin Bobby."

"No." he said thoughtfully, "I don't have any girl cousins that I know of."

"Maybe," Jennifer said laughing. "She was the daughter of the priest."

"All that time we went together, and I never knew you had a sense of humor."

"You never gave me a chance to kid around. All you ever wanted to do was fuck me," Jennifer whispered, a smile beginning in the corner of her mouth.

"You always said you liked it."

"I loved it. For a long time there, it was all I lived for. You were great. I'm just saying that I didn't have much time to laugh. Remember when we went to the orchard every night that one summer. My mom couldn't figure why I always wore a dress, instead of shorts or pants.

I didn't have the heart to tell her that it was easier because all you had to do was flip my dress up, pull down my panties, get behind me and do me doggie style. For a long time, there I was contemplating, learning how to bark.

Your mom always wondered how someone your age could have so many grass stains on the knees of his jeans. I would have told her, but I didn't want her to stop you from fucking me every night. We were lucky I didn't get pregnant. We did it a whole year until that time I missed my period, then you got some rubbers."

"You think we were lucky, that you didn't get pregnant? I wanted you to get pregnant in the worst way. I wanted to marry you. I was in love with you. I still am in love with you." His voice trailed off.

"I know Robert. Me too." Said Jennifer thoughtfully, looking into his eyes.

"Would you like something to drink?" He asked.

"Maybe a lemonade?"

Robert went over to the table where his mother was cooking. He picked up a lemonade and said,

"Mom I want to ask you about one of my baptism photos."

"Later Robert. I'm right in the middle of dinner."

"Mommm!"

"I said later Robert," cutting him off. "Later ...ok?"

"Ok mom."

He took the lemonade back to Jennifer and sat down next to her.

"What happened?" she asked."

Robert didn't say anything. He just looked at the photo and shook his head. Ten minutes later they all stared having dinner. After dinner, Eric suggested a game of horseshoes. He knew it was the only thing that would get his dad away from the TV. Sure enough when the shoes began striking the metal pins, Earl appeared at the back door.

"You guys playin' shoes?"

"Yah dad," said Eric. "Wanna' play?"

"Maybe for a little while."

They played for two hours and everyone was having a good time except Jim, who was sitting at the table talking on his cell phone and cussing out his estranged wife.

"Don't start bitchin' at me Erin. You were fucking that guy at your work, long before I ever started goin' out. Well fuck you too ... bitch."

Jim took the cell phone and jammed it down into the remaining potato salad, then sat there staring at nothing, mumbling under his breath.

"Hey Bro." Said Eric, "that's not good for the salad."

"Don't start with me Eric. Not now."

"Sorry Bro."

Jim just nodded his head, tears noticeably welling up in his eyes, a look of frustration on his face. His mother started in his direction when Earl said,

"Leave him alone Marge. He's not eight anymore."

"But Earl ..."

"I said leave him alone. He don't need no Goddamn motherin' now,"

"Bobby," said Jennifer. "Would you like to go for a ride?"

"I ... uh ... don't have a car."

"We can take mine. I have a little Nissan Z."

"Sure if you want."

Robert told his mother that he and Jennifer were going out for a ride and he would see them later. They went out to the front and cut across the lawn. Jennifer's sports car was parked in her mother's driveway.

"Where are your mom and dad?"

"They had to go to a business meeting?"

"You know that I hated them when they sent you to Texas."

"Yah, me too. You wanna' drive?"

"Sure, why not."

The sports car was a simple four on the floor, but Robert hadn't driven a stick in years. It took a few blocks, but then he was shifting like a Nascar pro. They moved out of the housing tract, then onto the Expressway.

The speed limit was seventy, but Robert had the little sports car up to eighty-two.

"Little sucker has some nags. What's it got, about two hundred horses?"

"Two-eighty-seven, and 3.5 liters." Said Jennifer. "When I need a quick orgasm, I just take it out on the highway and crank it up. It never fails me. Damn my panties are getting damp right now."

When Robert saw a Police car on the other side of the Expressway, he took his foot off the gas and backed down to sixty-five, then headed for the off ramp, in case the Police turned around. When he saw where they were, he realized they were almost twenty miles from their parent's houses.

"Go down this road," said Jennifer smiling.

"Why what's down there?"

"Just go."

Robert drove down the two-lane road and saw some lights up ahead. There was a gas station and a motel.

"Go in there."

"In the motel?" Asked Robert.

"Well not the gas station, I've got almost a full tank."

Robert sat there looking into Jennifer's beautiful green eyes, not sure what to do next.

"Do you have money?" asked Jennifer.

"Yah."

"Well go in and pay the woman for a room."

She had the same smile she had years past when they went to the orchard.

"A room?"

She again smiled, raised her eyebrows, nodding her head.

"Yes, a room Bobby. Although I am very horny right now, I'm not going to do it in the car like a couple of teenagers. Go on Bobby hurry up."

He got out of the little car unsure if everything was real. When he looked back at Jennifer, she motioned with her hand, fingers down as a teacher might do instructing a student to move on. As it was a Sunday night and there was only one car in the parking lot, Robert went into the motel office and a little old lady asked,

"Would you like a room young man?"

"Yes for two."

"You and your wife? Is that correct?" She glared at Robert.

"Yes ... my wife ... yes ... my wife and I ... thank you."

"Number six has a King-sized bed. Did you want a King-sized bed?"

"That would be fine. Thank you." Robert smiled.

"That will be Forty-five dollars and thirty-six cents, including tax. If you need help with your bags, I'll call my son."

"No ... no thanks I can handle them."

Robert handed her a Fifty-dollar bill. She handed him the key and some change. Robert was so excited he didn't even count it. As he got back in the car he said,

"Number Six."

Jennifer smiled and hooked her arm in his tightly, which made it a little difficult to shift, so he drove the fifty-foot distance slowly in first gear. He pulled the car up in front of room #6 and got out. Jennifer was already standing in front of the door, her hands clasp in front of her, like a little girl waiting for a treat at Halloween. Robert unlocked the door and Jennifer ran in making a dive and jumping onto the bed.

"Come here good lookin'. I want to play."

"Oh crap," said Robert.

"That's not very romantic, or sexy Robert."

"I didn't know this was going to happen, so I didn't bring any condoms."

"It seems like the guy is always the last to know." Said Jennifer letting out a little sigh. "Robert I'm on the "Super Pill".

"What's that?"

"It's the pill you take so when you wake up in the morning, and know that you're not pregnant, you yell "SUPER."

Jennifer was on her knees in her tight little white shorts, bouncing a little on the bed. Her green top clashed with the orange wallpaper, and large blue butterflies.

"You know Robert, this will only be the third time we will have done it in a bed. We did it once in your bed, when I snuck into your room through your window. Remember, your mother kept banging on your door asking, "Robert, what are you doing in there. All you could say was, nothing mom."

The second time was in my bed when my parents went out to an x rated movie, and you had to be twenty-one to get in. They should have just stayed at home and watched us. They could have saved the ten dollars."

She then pulled her top over her head, and pulled her shorts down, tossing them across the room. She was just in her matching yellow bra and panties.

"Do you like my new panties and bra? I got them just for you."

"Yah!" said Robert taking off his shoes. "What do you mean, you got them just for me?"

"Your mom told me two weeks ago that you were coming for a visit. You didn't think that I was at her house for her cooking, did you? I want your cock inside of me again Robert. I want you to lick my pussy, to make me cum like no other man ever has. I want you to fuck me until I bleed. Seduce me Bobby."

"What?"

"You know say something naughty, like you used to do when we were younger."

"Jennifer, I want to suck your breasts, and lick and suck your nipples. I'm going to take your clit in my mouth and..."

"Close enough. Come here. I'm burning up. I want you to fuck me like we used to do in the orchard ... doggie style."

By the time he tore off his shirt, and pulled down his pants, Jennifer was on her knees looking over her shoulder, panting,

"I'm waiting Bobby."

"In a second Jennifer." He said pulling off his jockeys and his socks.

"I can't wait a second. Come on."

Robert got behind her, took hold of her shiny black panties and pulled them down to her knees. Holding her hips tight he pushed forward, his cock sliding in between her slippery pussy lips. She groaned and said,

"I've missed you so much. Fuck me 'baby'."

He knew that he was home again, as "baby" was her pet name for Robert when they had gone together. Robert was feeling good. Better than he had in a long time. He had missed his chance when she went away to college, but now she knew what she wanted, and he wanted her.

Robert's cock was pushing deep into her pussy over and over again. Jennifer tried to talk dirty to him, but most of what she uttered were just moans and groans. He was moving fast, when he reached around and took hold of her boobs and squeezed them. She let out a muffled scream and climaxed hard bathing his cock and balls in her juice. This was the same Jennifer as the one he had dated when they were younger, a little older maybe, but just the same. He loved her, and he always would.

After the previous night at his brother's apartment, with the college girls, Robert was in no way ready to cum. He was really going to show her what she had missed. He felt a little guilty for the evening before, however that was a different time and a different world.

He was with the love of his life now, and he knew that she loved him. Only about thirty seconds had passed since Jennifer had cum. She was moaning loud and ready again. He wondered how long she had gone without sex. Her vagina emitted a gurgling sound, more juice and then she was crying.

Robert was really getting into it now. He asked,

"Why are you crying honey? Did I hurt you?"

"No, no, no, God it feels so good to have you in me again baby. I love you so much. I'm crying because I love you Bobby and I have missed you. Ooooo, God fuck me harder baby shove your giant cock up my pussy. Make me cum again, and then cum in me. I want to feel your hot cum squirting into my pussy. Please baby fill me up."

Apparently, her arms and legs wouldn't hold her up anymore and she slowly eased forward onto the bed lying prone on her stomach. Robert was right with her, still fucking her as hard and as fast as he could. He moved forward on her and began fucking her in a downward movement, so his cock would come in contact with her "G" spot. It worked and she came again. Now she was motionless and very quiet, so he stopped, his cock still hard. As he slipped out of her she moaned but said nothing.

Grabbing one of the small motel pillows, Robert bunched it up and pushed it under Jennifer's stomach causing her butt to elevate. He then pushed her knees apart and moved his face down between her butt cheeks.

Jennifer used to love it when he licked her cunt, constantly begging him for more. Her cute little puckered butt hole was right in front of his nose, as his tongue slid into her vagina, licking and tongue fucking her with it. She was beginning to come back to life and felt him draining the juice out of her.

His tongue was now coming in contact with her clitoris. She screamed into a pillow and began spraying his face. She was in heaven, fucking heaven. Robert slid his arms between her legs and under her thighs almost lifting her off the bed. His strong arms came around, and his hands grabbed her butt.

He thought it almost looked like a couple of naked wrestlers in some kind of a weird hold that hadn't been done before. As his fingers took hold of her cheeks, and he spread her open, he poked his tongue into her butt hole. This was something he had never done, but the way she screamed he was sure she liked it.

As Robert was holding her up, almost upside down, his lips took hold of her swollen engorged clitoris. He sucked on "the little man in the boat" as though it was a small penis. Her vagina began pumping, opening and closing as though it was groping for his cock. Moving his legs out from under her he laid on his back not letting her go, still sucking on her clit and pussy lips.

Jennifer was lost in the fantastic lust he was providing. She had never had sex like this before, even with Robert. She was lying flat on his stomach, and she saw that his cock was pointing toward the ceiling. Jennifer slowly took hold of it with both hands. Pulling it Robert thought she was going to jack him off, however she did something she had never done in the past. She slipped the head of his cock into her mouth and began sucking lightly.

"Honey you don't have to do that. You never wanted too before."

Removing her mouth for a few seconds, she licked up and down the engorged shaft, causing Robert to groan. She said,

"Baby, if you love me enough to stick your tongue in my butt, I can suck your cock; besides I really like the way it feels in my mouth."

Jennifer licked it again, this time from his balls to the end of his cock.

"Damn," she said. "Why didn't I do this when we were going together?"

A Nun's Tale

"You thought it was gross."

"I was young and dumb. I'm sorry baby."

His cock again disappeared into her mouth and she sucked harder, as Robert slid his tongue into her bright red pussy. He was fascinated as her vagina was making involuntary contractions apparently attempting to suck his tongue into its depths.

Her vagina was doing the same thing to Robert's tongue that her mouth was doing to his cock. All he really had to do was just relax, as if any guy could relax with a beautiful girl who had her mouth on his penis. He was beginning to get that devastating feeling again, the one he had experienced so many times in the orchard.

He felt it his back, a slight pain but a good pain. He then felt a tightening in his balls. She was going to make him cum in her mouth. He couldn't believe it. When they were younger, he would have never have suggested it. Suddenly she stopped, raised her head and moaned loudly. Her sweet delectable juices began dribbling out of her pussy. He sucked them up and moved his mouth all around her saturated slippery pussy lips, causing her to be at the height of her pleasure. She groaned again and more liquid came dribbling out.

"Wait ... wait ... Jesus Bobby!"

Now it was like she was frozen in time, not moving, her discharge oozing down from her pink pussy on to his mouth and chin. He hesitated, knowing he had pushed her over some sexual precipice, and she didn't want to move for the fear of what was yet to come. He pulled one arm free and very slowly, pushed a finger into her swollen vagina, saturating it.

"God no baby ... wait."

Pulling his finger free, Robert slowly entered her sphincter to his second knuckle, and then began to finger fuck her ass.

"Aaaaaaaaa." She cried in a high-pitched voice. That had done it. It had been like opening floodgates on a dam. He thought for just a second she was peeing, but the unmistakable viscosity and the taste of her delightful juice, couldn't be urine. She was climaxing like he had never witnessed before.

Her orgasm could go into the "Gunnies World Book" thought Robert. He now knew that his little girl was a complete woman. She slumped forward, not letting go of his swollen penis. She had wanted to complete what she had been doing to him, but he couldn't have incapacitated her more if he had struck her on her chin and knocked her out.

It was fine. His selfishness had paid off. More than anything in the world he had wanted to pleasure her, and he had done it. No matter what occurred from that time on, Robert knew sex would never be the same for his little girl. He had pushed all of her love buttons, and she was out.

After ten minutes her juice had slowed down to an occasional drip. She had not moved however, so he knew that he had to make the effort. Although he was enjoying the little sucking pulsating show her vagina was performing for him, he knew they couldn't spend the next several hours in this position.

First, he slowly moved her sculptured legs to the left, and eased out from under her a little. He stopped for a few seconds as not to startle her. Then he very slowly pulled his legs free and moved away from her on the bed.

As Robert lay next to her, staring at her, he thought she looked like a Renoir painting, only a little thinner. He smiled as he felt Renoir would have given his left nut to paint such a lovely sight. Her ass was gorgeous. At least as nice as any he had ever seen in playboy. He loved her beautiful ass.

Chapter 3

Although he felt deep empathy for her condition, Robert's cock was extremely hard, and he knew his balls were turning the color of the butterflies on the wall. They were filled with cum and he was in some serious pain. He wondered if fucking her at that moment would be adding insult to injury.

"I'm sorry honey, but I can't take it anymore."

Robert's words fell on deaf ears however. As he moved on top of her, he saw her cute little butt. The butt of his dreams, he thought. Placing one knee on the outside of her left thigh, he swung his right leg over; as he had seen many cowboys do in the movies.

He was now sitting astride her looking down at her beautiful rear end. Between her cheeks, her pussy was still dripping and oozing the cream of total satisfaction. But now it was his turn. He took hold of his penis and guided it into her still pulsing vagina.

As she realized what was occurring, she moaned,

"No baby ... it's too much ... wait ... wait a minute."

Robert could not wait any longer and moved forward plunging his cock into her. She groaned again as the tip of his penis came in contact with her cervix. It felt wonderful and she shifted her hips up to help him, as much as she could in her condition.

Robert appreciated her efforts however; he needed no help. Everything was there. The girl he had always loved, who had loved him. His hard penis and her dripping pussy; and most of all a screaming need in his brain to fuck her and shoot all of his hot cum deep into her.

It was a delectable feeling, and he moved very slowly at first. He smiled, as she would let out a little groan each time, he shoved into her. The feeling began to be overwhelming, and he was now moving with mechanical precision. He was again fucking his girlfriend as he had done countless times in the past, and she was beginning to respond.

"Oh God; oh God; oh God," she muttered almost in a whisper. "Fuck me Bobby, fuck me hard baby. I need you."

Robert had pulled so hard on her pelvis that she was now up on her knees and pushing her butt back into him with all of her remaining strength. His perspiration was running off of his forehead and splashing on Jennifer's back. She felt it and cried out as it though it was acid. They were no longer Jennifer and Robert, two separate entities. They had come together, and they were one.

He had heard the priest say the words at several weddings, however until this moment the real meaning had eluded him. Now he understood. They were two persons attached though a symbiotic like relationship, and had become one, relying on each other for the extreme pleasure no other persons could provide them.

Robert again felt the back pain, the tingling in his thighs and his balls tightening as though they were in velvet vice. All of the signs were there, and relief was eminent. Just as Robert's sperm was forcing its way toward the tip of his cock, Jennifer expelled an ear-piercing scream, which was closely followed by a sound that Robert thought at first was a firecracker exploding in her vagina.

He quickly realized that she had the mother of all orgasms. Neither of them moved for several moments. He was holding her hips, as though the two of them were connected. At that point she was unconcerned with the world and hugged her pillow like a little girl, ready for dreamland.

With a resounding "Uhhhhhhh" from Jennifer's lips, due to her strong and uncontrollable desire for him to remain inside of her, a painful emptiness in her vagina was created when he pulled his cock free.

He then helped her lay down on her stomach, and as she was so wet from his perspiration, he covered her with the sheet, which began to soak up all of the moisture. Lying down next to her, he thought of the many painful nights and days he had been without her.

He smiled to himself knowing things would be different now. She was his totally and would remain that way until his dying day. As Robert lay back, the wonderfully satisfaction of sex induced sleep overtook him. She had made him complete.

Robert awakened to a dream of a little frightened girl of eight crying, in what looked to be a dark damp basement. She was tied to a chair, her arms and legs bound with towels. He sat up in bed, looking around realizing that he and Jennifer were still at the motel. His heart was beating rapidly, due to the dream and his movements had awakened Jennifer to a state between sleep and consciousness.

Robert sat up against the bed board, recalling the dream in its entirety. He seemed to recall having the dream before, or had it been a reality, he couldn't be sure. However, he was sure that there was a part of the dream that was missing.

"God." Said Jennifer, in an unintelligible Midwestern Ohio accent. "Were you trying to kill me Robert, because you almost succeeded? I don't think my arms and legs work anymore. What time is it anyway?"

"Two in the morning," said Robert, glancing at the digital clock on the TV set, its large red letters illuminating the room, turning some of the wallpaper butterflies purple.

"Come here Robert and cuddle up, so we can sleep a little more."

Robert moved down and cuddled with his girl, hoping the dream would not return. Although he knew it had not been about him, he hadn't been quite that frightened in a long time. He was a little scared to go back to sleep, so he laid there planning their future.

He knew that he had enough in the bank for a down payment on a modest home in Santa Barbara. There were new houses being built near Parma Park, with wonderful views of the Pacific Ocean. They were still young enough to have a child of their own; and maybe even two.

It would be a great family. Her two kids and one or two of their own. He would leave it up to her, as she was the one who would suffer the discomfort of pregnancy and the pain of childbirth. The only thing holding them back was her divorce.

Robert awoke at five o'clock, just as the dawn was chasing away the night. He had a strange feeling. He was on his back naked and Jennifer was on her knees by his midsection, her mouth on his penis, sucking him.

"What ... what's ..."

She removed he mouth from his cock, however continued to jack him off and asked,

"I'm sorry, did I wake you? It just looked so tasty, I wanted to try again."

"Please," said Robert. "Please continue."

Jennifer smiled, and then went back to her chore of draining Robert's testicles. He laid back, closed his eyes and enjoyed what she was doing. He thought heaven would never be like this. All of the angels would be ironing their sheets, dusting clouds, having their halos charged and polished. He would probably the one assigned to throwing lightning bolts down to earth. But there wouldn't be any sex.

Then he thought, what if there was sex in heaven? He could see a supervisor angel sitting at a large marble table, a gigantic book opens in front of him, his head in his hands. Standing in front of him, a cute little blonde angel looking embarrassed with a big pregnant belly. The supervisor says,

"A perfect record shot to hell!"

He felt it and opened his eyes. It was coming. He could feel it in his thighs and back and now in his balls.

"Sweetie wait ... take your mouth off. I'm cuming."

Jennifer held up a hand, like a crossing guard stopping traffic and continued to suck, even harder if that was possible. No more warning he thought and let go of his sperm. It shot into her mouth hard and she sat up with a surprised look on her face. Her cheeks were puffed out like she had a mouth full of water. But it wasn't water, and it appeared as though she wasn't sure what to do with it.

"Spit it out honey. You don't have to swallow it."

She shook her head "no" then gulped. She smiled at Robert then like a little girl who had taken all of her medicine, she opened her mouth wide to show him.

"Did you like it?" he asked tentatively.

"Wasn't bad. I could get used to it if you wanted me too. I really liked the feeling of your penis in my mouth though. It was like sucking on a whole pepperoni, only not quite as spicy. Kind of stretched my out mouth though." She said exercising her jaw. "I only have one question," she said smiling and licking her lips. "Does this make me a cannibal?"

Robert laughed and shook his head. Jennifer moved over next to him and lay on her back. She said in a squeaky little girl voice,

"Mister I sucked your lollypop, now it's your turn to lick my pee-pee."

Robert said nothing and crawled over to her. As he was at her feet, he took one foot in each hand and moved them out almost to arm's length. She was spread open and her pussy was very pretty and waiting for him. He eased down until his face was within licking distance, of her and said,

"Put your legs on my shoulders honey."

"Ok mister, what are you going to do? She asked still using the little girl voice.

"You'll see,"

He began kissing the insides of her thighs, and then licked them with long wet strokes of his tongue, much like a cocker spaniel would do licking his own balls. He knew that he was making progress, when a severe pain came to his scalp. Jennifer was moaning and pulling his hair with both hands. He made a mental note to tell her at a later time, that he would soon be bald if she didn't show a little restraint.

He had always loved the look of her pussy. She had never had any pubic hair, and he hadn't asked her why. It wasn't a bad thing as far as he was concerned, as he loved to have his mouth on her as much as she would let him, and he believed the hair would have just been in the way.

Her little lips were always tightly tucked into the major ones, making a perfect slit, except of course when he went down on her. Then her inner lips would swell up and display themselves, inviting him in.

The taste of her pussy was almost indiscernible. Delicious was the only word that could be used. If there had been enough calories to sustain his life, he would give up food totally and gorged himself at her fountain of lust, at the very least three times a day.

Robert had always liked a little cream in his coffee, however he was less than satisfied, as it didn't taste like Jennifer's cream. He moved his tongue to the juncture between her leg and her pussy lips. He knew she would be almost insane with anticipation for his mouth and his tongue to enter the area she saved only for him.

"Please Robert," she begged, "Please."

Robert knew what she needed and wanted so bad. He moved his lips to her slit, which was now wide open and very moist. His mouth opened and covered all of her inner lips and clitoris. He began to suck and revel in her pussy like a young boy eating a juicy pomegranate. Her pussy was at least as sweet and tangy, as the ripe fruit would be. Moving his attention to her swollen engorged clit, Robert began to suck on the little penis like form, wishing it had been just a little larger so he could really put his lips around it.

Jennifer screamed and sprayed his chin with her juice, but knowing how much she needed gratification, and his attention, he continued. It had been his goal to pleasure her, as much as possible from the time he found out that he could. It was always a wonderful feeling for him to make Jennifer the center of his world.

He placed his hands under her smooth knees, in back of her thighs and lifted her legs so they were almost hanging in space. This movement brought her beautiful vagina into view, and only a few inches lower was her little butt hole, which was winking at him invitingly.

He first licked slowly from her winking little hole, up to her tight vagina sucking all the way. Then with the daring of an Acapulco cliff diver he dove into her pussy hole, tongue first. Due to the God's lack of understanding, and knowledge of most mortal's fanatical love of cunnilingus, they failed to give the male of the species a tongue, long enough to make a real difference. Robert always felt men should have been equipped with the tongue of an aardvark, only just for vaginas and not ants. He continued pumping his tongue as deep as it would go.

Occasionally Robert would pull his tongue out and suck hard on whatever was swollen and available, especially her lips and clit. He would then slide his slippery serpent back into its sheath, moving it deep, in an impossible quest to reach her cervix.

Jennifer flexed and gritted her teeth, as her vagina attempted to grab Robert's tongue. All the muscles of her body were flexed, as a severe pain traveled from her back to her belly then down to her pussy. She was in extreme pain until a flood of pleasure came in erasing the pain and leaving her in an almost supernatural state. The feeling was so overpowering that she almost believed she was communicating with God.

Robert knew that what she required was his version of tender loving care. He laid there his mouth on her open dripping pussy, slowly nursing on her labia and clitoris as a small baby might do at its mother's breasts. His older brother had taught him well when he said,

"Robert, if you are goanna' go to the trouble of goin' down on a broad, make sure you keep it up until she passes out, or it just ain't worth it, 'cause if she dosen't pass out ... she's going to be frustrated and want to talk."

Jennifer was almost at that point. As he slowly sucked her clitoris, she gushed fluids which seemed to him were coming out in spoonsful. He looked up at her face. She was out.

It was eight forty-five in the morning and Jennifer hadn't moved a hair in several hours. As check out was at ten, Robert went into the bathroom to take a shower. He came out naked, drying with a tiny towel provided by the motel and sat on the side of the bed. Reaching over, he touched her face and whispered,

"Sweetheart its time to get up."

A Nun's Tale

Jennifer frowned, still not opening her eyes, much like she had when her mother woke up to go to school.

"Jennifer Ann Conley," Robert said in a high-pitched voice attempting to emulate her mother, "It's time to get up."

She opened one eye halfway, then the other, a deep frown on her face, squinting at Robert. Although she didn't want to get out of bed, she was pleased that he had awakened her, as she had been having a dream that she was "Snow White" and two of the seven dwarfs had been looking for diamonds in her vagina.

"Come on you have to take a shower, or your mother will know that you have been fucking like a horny little monkey."

"I have been fucking like a horny little monkey, and I don't want to get up."

"Didn't you tell me that you have the swing shift at the Hospital at two o'clock?"

"It's not two o'clock yet."

"No but you have to take a shower. We have to go to breakfast, and then you have to drop me at my parent's house. After that you have to get a uniform and drive fifteen miles to work."

"That's too much Robert. You do it," she said in her defiant little girl's voice.

"Do what?"

"You go to work for me."

"I can't," he said, "My legs are too hairy, and I have a mustache."

"Shave!"

"Shave my mustache?"

"Yes, and your legs too. I'll wait here for you. We can do it all over again tonight."

"Get up and take a shower ... Jennifer Ann ... now!" he stated with authority.

"Oooohhh kay."

Jennifer got off the giant bed and walked toward the bathroom naked, dragging her feet like an eight-year-old, who had been told that it was time for bed. It was all Robert could do to restrain himself from grabbing her and fucking her in the shower. She spent thirty minutes under the warm pulsating water. When she came out, she looked shiny, like a newly minted quarter.

"I can't find my panties," she said, looking under the bed.

As she bent over Robert could have sworn that her vagina winked at him.

"Here they are," he said as he swung them around his index finger.

"What are you doing with my panties?"

"I was sniffing them."

"You dirty little boy. I'm going to tell your mother."

"What? I can spend countless hours with my mouth in your pussy, but I can't sniff your panties?"

She smiled at him. "Thank you Robert, that was some of your best work. I just wish I had been there at the end. I think I passed out. You were so wonderful."

She sat on the side of the bed and slipped into her yellow panties then her bra and her green top. After that she put her socks and shoes on, she got off the bed and walked over to him where he was seated on a chair. She was dressed except for her tight white shorts.

She stood in front of him, turned around, bent over and wiggled her butt in his face. That was all he could take. She wasn't going to get away with that. He got out of the chair, wrapped his arms around her waist and carried her over to the bed. He pushed her on to the bed, bending over it with her feet on the floor.

"What are you doing? We have to leave. Look at the time."

Quickly he pulled her panties down to her ankles, while simultaneously, pulling his own pants and underpants down. She looked around and seeing his erection she said,

"Mr. English, what are you doing?"

"You will soon find out what happens to a tease."

He moved in closer to her gorgeous bare butt, pulled her cheeks open with his thumbs and shoved his cock into her pussy. Grabbing her hips, he pulled her toward him and began fucking her very hard and very rough.

Jennifer grabbed a pillow and some of the blankets, as she knew that she was in for a violent and turbulent ride. She was surprised as Robert had never taken her by force, but she liked it. It was kind of nice to be "raped a little" by somebody you loved. She knew of course that it was her fault. Not many men could take that kind of teasing.

She wondered how long it would take for him to cum, as they were on a time limit. But now it was beginning to feel so good, she didn't care if they were late or not. Robert could really fuck her, and she loved every second of it. He had been in the shower not too long before, so he was beginning to sweat, but this was so great he just didn't care.

"God Bobby; it's so good. Fuck me harder."

'How ... he thought, didn't she know that he had already thrown everything he had into it?'

His knees were getting weak, so he leaned into the bed and braced himself, then pulled harder on her hips.

"Robert ... I'm going to cum. Cum with me baby. Squirt in my pussy. Uuuuhhh."

He felt Jennifer discharge and was about to cum himself when somebody knocked on the motel room door.

"In ... a ... minute." He called, "In ... a ... minute."

His cum began to squirt into her pussy, and fought with her juice, which was trying to get out and coat her raw vagina. The knocking repeated and Robert finally ask in a sex strained irritated voice,

"Yes, what is it?"

The little old lady's voice cracked as she called through the dark blue door,

"Check out time is ten o'clock."

"We know. Thank you," he said as the last of his cum shooting into Jennifer's cunt.

A Nun's Tale

As he began to pull his cock out of her vagina, he looked at the clock. It displayed nine forty. 'Damn he thought, he still had an erection. Well he wasn't about to stop now.'

Grabbing her hips harder, he shoved back into his lover and began to fuck her again. She couldn't believe it. He had already cum, but wasn't finished yet?

"What are you doing Robert, going for a gold metal? Baby I won't be able to walk to the car."

"I'll carry you."

Well she knew better than argue when he had an erection. She grabbed the pillow again and held on. She was still on cloud nine from the fucking he had just given her, so it didn't look like he was going to let her down soon. Robert ignored her remarks and shoved harder and faster, attempting to beat the clock and cum again before they had to leave.

Unbelievably she was again getting into it. Two minutes had passed, and she was going to cum again. She thought as her climax was overtaking her, he must have studied hard for this. After she came yet again, she said,

"Why did you make me take a shower, when you knew that you were going to get me all dirty again."

She felt like she was in a Supermarket, and some guy behind her kept bumping into her cart, but in a very nice way. What did this man eat; was it vitamins, large steaks or salads. His endurance was unbelievable and wonderful. She thought about calling in sick, after all she was completely worn out. He looked at the clock. Nine minutes to ten. Robert moved his hips faster, his forehead soaked from perspiration.

She had no idea that she was really involved in this final attack on her body, however, her vagina was again responding to his relentless pumping and again she began to cum.

Robert, out of breath and out of strength, fired off the last of his sperm into his lovely partner's pussy, believing it would be days before his penis would voluntarily peek out of its hiding place.

In a hurry they got dressed again and exited the motel room. The little old lady was standing by the door, tapping her foot. As they entered her car, Jennifer said, looking at her watch,

"We still have three minutes, wanna' go back?"

Robert smiled and then backed the little car out of the parking space.

"I'm sorry Jen did you want to drive?"

"Oh sure, like I could."

They drove slowly down the road, looking for a restaurant. They were both starved and dehydrated, craving liquid and sustenance. It was a beautiful morning, and the sky ahead was blue and clear, however as a metaphor, that would not last for very long. Jennifer spotted a restaurant.

"There's one," she said pointing out the window.

"That's a 'Skyline Chili' restaurant. They don't serve breakfast."

"I don't care," said Jennifer, "I'm hungry and they have food."

"Yah chili."

"Chili is food. Pull in Robert."

A Nun's Tale

The restaurant had just opened at ten thirty and they were the first customers. A woman dressed in a uniform said,

"Sit anywhere, I'll be right with you."

They sat in a booth, and stared at each other for several seconds, then burst into laughter.

"You think that little old lady was pissed?" ask Jennifer.

"Probably, but not because of the time. She was pissed 'cause she can't do what we do so well."

"Yah! What do you think my pussy is, your personal storage locker?"

Robert shook his head from side to side. "Uh, uh. Storage lockers are cold, and you are really hot."

"You know that my pussy is still buzzing. Feels like I left a vibrator in there and forgot to turn it off."

"Thank you, I think."

"Absolutely. You are wonderful but you can slow down just a little. You have me totally convinced. Do you remember the movie with Frank Sinatra, where he was a drummer on drugs?"

"Man, with the Golden Arm?"

"Yah ... well they are going to make a movie about you. "The man with the Golden Cock." You and I can do all of the love scenes.

The waitress came over to their table and said,

"We got good chili."

"Hence the name?" said Robert.

"What?" asked the waitress? Robert shook his head.

"Jennifer said, "I'll take a bowl of chili, without beans. Gas you know." She smiled.

The waitress paid no attention and asked,

"Oyster or regular?"

"Excuse me?" asked Jennifer narrowing her eyebrows.

"Oyster crackers or regular crackers." She stated slowly almost spelling it out.

"Oyster please, and hurry."

"Drink?"

"Coke?"

When the waitress looked at Robert, and he began to laugh hysterically and said,

"I'll have the same, no onions, and no ice in the coke please."

The waitress looked at Robert, thinking that he may be out of the Loony bin on a break, and then turned on her heals to put in the order. Robert had laughed as his sweet little unassuming girlfriend, had grabbed his cock when it had been his turn to order.

"Don't do that." He said.

"Why not? It belongs to me."

The waitress returned with their order.

"Quick enough for ya?"

"Thank you," said Jennifer. When the waitress left, she said, "There goes her tip."

As they ate Jennifer talked all about Robert's superhuman abilities and the fact that he should wear a red cape to warn girls that he was coming. Then she changed subjects and expounded on the fabulous taste of his semen, sounding like some Hollywood gay fruit loop who had just returned from a blind date.

"Robert are you still horny?"

"No." he stated looking at here in disbelief.

<u>Chapter 4</u>

"I want you to go home and sit in a cold tub and pack your balls with ice. Then I want you to take a nap so you will be ready for me when I get off work. I'll be home at ten thirty. I'll meet you in the orchard at ten forty-five. OK?"

"You are kidding?"

"Ten forty-five. Be there with bells, or balls on. Don't let me down."

"We can get another motel room, if you want Jess?"

"No, I want to do it in the orchard. I always loved it when we fucked under all of the trees."

The waitress was just passing when she heard the word "fucked" and stood there with her mouth hanging open."

Jessica looked back at her flashing her gorgeous green eyes, smiling and asked in her little girl voice,

"Don't you fuck?"

The waitress dropped the check on the table as if she were doing them a favor, then turned and walked away.

"Bitch," Jessica muttered under her breath, "Like she never had her pussy stretched out a little."

Robert pulled into Jessica's parent's driveway and after kissing her on her bee stung lips; he got out of her car. She looked at him seriously and asked.

"Where are you going to be at 10:45 tonight?"

Robert pointed toward the back yard. Jess nodded her head and said,

"Apple tree, right? Don't keep me waiting."

"I'll be there. Are you sure you are OK to go to work?"

"Yes, but I'm going to take another shower first ... you wild horny devil. I love it. Now go some rest. I want you fresh when I get home. I just hope I'll be able to move around tonight at work. I'm going to try and work in admissions so I can give "your" little pussy a rest. Don't forget the ice.

Robert dragged himself into his parent's house and flopped on the couch. His mother who was just finishing "All my Children" asked how he was felling after their long ride.

"I'm ok mom, just a little tired."

"That must have been some ride Robert."

"It was mom; it really was."

"Where did you go?"

"Just beyond Jupiter and back." He said in a monotone voice.

"That's nice. It's good to get out once in a while."

"Mom I want to talk about the little girl in the photo."

"I'm sorry Robert, I'm so busy, maybe before you leave."

"What are you so busy doing? When I came in you were just finishing your soap opera."

"They are daytime dramas Robert."

"A rose by any other name mom."

"What?"

"Nothing mom. Get the book I want to talk about the girl. Who is she?"

"Robert, it's really none of your business."

"Is Eric home?"

"No he's at the Gym. Why?"

"I'm leaving mom and I'll need a ride to the station." He lied.

"Why Robert," she asked almost in tears.

"Well let's face it. If as you say, it is really none of my business, this is not my family, and I have to go. I'll be out in an hour."

"Please don't go Robert. I haven't seen you in years and I don't know when I'll see you again, living all the way out there in Saint Harbor."

"Santa Barbara, mom. I'll stay if you will tell me all about the little girl and leave nothing out. Otherwise I'll call a cap and I'm out of here," said Robert grabbing the phone.

She got up with a groan, due to her heavy weight, and walked over to the cabinet that was the sanctuary where she kept all of the family photos. She slowly came back and then asked Robert if he wanted something to drink.

"Quit stalling mom."

She sat down with another heavy sigh and asked, "Why do you want to know. It's all in the past."

"I want to know, because you have been hiding it from me for so long, and because you are making it so difficult."

"OK ... but you won't be happy about it."

"Just get the photos out mom."

She opened the book to the section where Robert was being baptized and moved her hand over the plastic covered photo caressing it, with love in her heart and tears in her eyes.

"Robert, I have something serious to tell you and I think you are going to hate me for it."

"Why did you kill someone?" He quipped.

"No ... worse."

"I don't think there is anything worse than killing someone, except maybe killing two people."

"Don' be flippant Robert. It's not funny ... I had a baby out of wedlock."

"Who was it ... me?"

"No ... your half-sister."

"Half-sister ... when?"

"I had just graduated high school. The priest in our parish knew our family needed money, and even though I wasn't really qualified, he got me a job at the seminary college. Everything went well for about three months; however brother Michael was so nice to me and so cute. He had a wonderful since of humor and ... "

"I understand mom. You fell in love and nature took its course."

"That's right Robert," she was feeling better about herself, and said, "Sometimes three times a night."

"I really don't need all of the details mom."

"Well you asked."

"Yes, about my sister."

"She is in Colorado at a Catholic school and she is very happy there."

"Why did you send her away?"

"When she was about eight, she began to play with herself ... down there ... you know, her private parts.

"She was masturbating?"

"Don't say that word Robert, it's just nasty."

"It's just a word mom. Most people do it."

"I don't want to hear that talk from you. Please stop it."

"OK. So, you little eight year old daughter, right of the blue began to play with her pus ..."

"Robert," his mother stopped him from saying the word.

"Mom, I've seen cases like this. Little girls don't begin doing it on their own. Someone molested her mom."

"Are you crazy?" Nobody did that. She started it on her own. That's all there is to it."

"Is it? Did she ever do anything like that before you married Earl?"

"No." his mother refused to look him in the eyes.

It was now clear to Robert. He remembered the dream; it was no dream at all. When Robert went down to the basement to get his dad, he saw the girl tied to a chair. His dad was in front of her, but he couldn't see what was going on. Earl yelled at him to "get the fuck out", so he did.

"Your father was drunk, and Katie was always coming on to him."

"She came on to him at eight years old. Is that why he tied her up?"

"He was drunk." She began crying.

"That's no excuse. Where is she now?"

"In Colorado."

"Exactly where in Colorado. She looked in the back pocket of the book and handed him a piece of paper.

"OK thanks mom. I know it was difficult for you ... but, I had to know. And mom I don't think less of you, and I still love you."

"Robert you must understand," she sobbed," I had two little boys and a new baby. I couldn't handle it alone."

"No matter what happened, it wasn't right for dad to do that."

Robert went into the back yard, just to think. He had a sister five years older than him. He just couldn't believe it. He wondered how she looked, how she talked. Why didn't he remember her around the house when he was little? His head was swimming. Should he call the police? The statute of limitations for child molestation ran out years ago, and Earl was almost seventy. What would be the point? It just wasn't right though. Somebody should have shot him. Everything Earl had put his mother through; Robert had never hated his father more.

Eric came out staring at his hand and his extend middle finger.

"I don't understand Bro. Why does my finger sticking up like that mean for someone to go fuck themselves?"

"It doesn't really Eric, do you know anything about the battle of Agincourt?

"No!" I didn't do well in Political Science."

"History little brother. Well during the battle, in 1415, the French, believed they would win a victory over the English, and several of their generals decided that whenever they captured an English longbow soldier they were going to cut off his middle finger, as without the finger it would be almost impossible to draw the renowned English longbow and they wouldn't be able to fight in the future either." "Yah and so ...?"

"The English longbow was made of the English Yew tree. The act of drawing the longbow was known as "Plucking the Yew", or pluck yew. Well the English defeated the French; and stood on the top of a hill above Agincourt, waiving their middle fingers at the defeated French, yelling see we can still pluck yew.

Over time "pluck yew" was changed into "Fuck You" and is often used with the single finger waive. 'Flipping the bird' came from the fact that pheasant feathers were used on the ends of the arrows. That's about it."

"How did you get so smart Bro?"

"You know those books that you carry from class to class?"

"Yah!"

"I read them."

"Ohhhh. Robert do you think you can teach me something?"

"I don't know. What little Brother?"

"e's mails."

"You mean e-mail?"

"Yah I guess."

"Why Eric?"

"Well at school, three or four girls have stopped me in the hallway and in class and asked me why I haven't answered their e-mails. So, I thought maybe 'cause you are so smart you could teach me."

"I guess I could try, come on."

The brothers went into the house, where their father was sleeping in his chair, waiting for a game to come on. Their mother was running what looked to be a pre second world war Hoover vacuum cleaner, which was as loud as any Second World War bomber. Robert asked his mother,

"Mom would you mind?"

"What Robert," she asked cupping her ear.

Robert pulled the electric cord out of the wall, and there was a dead silence. His father woke up and asked,

"Is the game on?"

"No Earl," said Marge, "I'll wake you in about forty-five minutes."

"And bring me a beer."

"Yes Earl, and none of that damned light beer either," she said.

"Right." Said Earl as he fell back to sleep.

Robert pushed the button on the front of the steal gray DELL, then pushed the on button for the monitor. The computer began to whir and the screen turned a bright blue. Several seconds later the word welcome was displayed toward the top of the monitor.

"What did you do Robert?" Eric said obviously impressed.

"I turned it on Eric."

"Ooohh! So, what's next?"

"You will see."

The tick, tick, tick of an old Westclox, wall clock was clicking the time away, reminding Robert how long it would be until Jennifer would be home. Robert only hoped he could pound the rudiments of the e-mail into Eric's head by that time.

Sitting behind Eric and off to his left he pointed out the start button and explained its purpose. As Eric placed the arrow key over the button a small sign in a yellow box came up and displayed,

"Click here to begin."

"Thanks Bro that wasn't too hard."

"We're not quite done yet Eric."

"There's more? Eric asked, with a frown, "Aw man."

"You want to read your mail, or not? Ok ... click on the start button."

A list of applications came up, on a gray background. Robert pointed to the icon that showed, E-Mail, Outlook Express, and told his little brother to click on it.

Four boxes of various sizes displayed filling the whole screen. The inbox was dark blue and had the number forty-six next to it in blue parentheses.

"You have forty-six e-mail messages."

"Forty-six. Shit that will take a hundred years ta' read."

"There not book length Eric. Some of them are only one or two sentences long. Click on that one."

An e-mail identified as Shelley Davis came up. It read,

"Eric, I'm metaphorically throwing my panties at you through Cyber space."

"What's that word Robert?

"Metaphorically?" asked Robert, "It means generally a figure of speech in which a word or phrase that ordinarily designates one thing is used to designate another, making an implicit comparison."

"What the fuck did you just say?"

"Uh ... it means she wants you to fuck her Eric."

"Well why didn't she just say that?"

"It has something to do with college."

"I'll click on the next one."

"Who is Linda Edwards, Eric?"

"She is my English teacher, probably wants to tell me about my English assignment."

The e-male read,

"Eric, my loins grow cold without the warmth of your massive phallus probing their depths."

Eric looked at his brother with a question on his face. Robert said,

"She wants you to fuck her."

"Oh yah, I guess it has been a couple of weeks."

Robert now saw his little brother in a new light. He was like "Johnny Appleseed", but instead of spreading seeds all over, he was spreading sperm. They went on to check the inbox, and except for one advertisement for electronic equipment, all the messages were from girls. Robert thought, this was a Cornucopia of women all wanting to fuck him, how was Eric ever going to keep up?

The one that really got their attention was from Susan James; it read; I just creamed my panties thinking about you Eric. I need to go to bed and rub on my happy spot, which is throbbing for attention right now. Wish you were here sucking my clit at the same time you were finger fucking my pussy with two fingers at once; maybe even three. Uum. I could cum all over your face and hand. I would suck your cock to help with your sexual relief too--then you could cum on my titties, ok!!

"Who is this Susan James, Eric?"

"Don't know. Never met her. She writes good though."

The time was up and so was their dad. With a beer in one hand and the remote in the other, he was yelling at a bunch of guys on TV playing basketball.

"OK brother, now comes the hard part. Answering your mail."

Robert went through all of the fine points of "Reply" showing Eric how it worked, then told him to start writing back.

Eric began by looking for the key marked "D" on the keyboard. He typed,

D ... e ... a ... r ... S ... u ... s ...a ... n,

"Hey Robert, this isn't bad. I can answer these letters."

Robert thought Eric was kidding when he said a hundred years, but now understood it was a ballpark figure. He thought about Eric's dilemma for a few moments then said,

"Common little Brother we are going to the Electronic Supermarket."

Upon their return to the house Robert got the package out and plugged it into the back of the computer. He then placed a CD application disk into the slot and waited. The screen came up with an install window and began to ask questions. When it was all done ten minutes later it said, Program Installed.

"Ok Eric, now we have to run a voice recognition program, so the computer will recognize your voice when you talk. Robert began with "Alice in Wonderland." Eric read the words as they displayed on the monitor. Then they went to "The three pigs" to which Eric stated,

"I like that one."

After two hours of drilling the process, in the middle of their dad's basketball game, into Eric's head, Robert saw that he finally got it, and was able to talk to the computer like anyone else.

Now whenever you and mom want to send me an e-mail, all you have to do is talk into the computer and send it. Eric was thrilled and got down to answering his fan mail. Robert wished teaching Eric everything else was as easy.

It was now almost five o'clock so he told his mother to wake him later around eight. He wanted to take a shower and be ready for Jennifer.

Robert step outside into the back yard, at ten thirty. He was pleased that it wasn't really cold, it was an almost warm balmy night and Robert had brought a blanket just in case. He ducked through the opening in the hurricane fence that he had made when he began going with Jennifer, and crawled through. When he arrived at the apple tree, Robert spread out the blanket and lay down.

As he lay there thinking of their earlier times together, he smelled the aromas of all the various trees. He recalled when his mother would pack him a lunch and place an apple inside; he would on occasion get a hard on just smelling it.

Hearing a noise of someone walking toward him, he looked up and saw Jennifer. She was wearing her old Catholic School uniform. She looked much younger than she actually was, maybe sixteen he thought. Jennifer sat down on the blanket and kissed him.

"What's wrong Jenn?"

"I miss my children. If I don't see them every day, I get a knot in my stomach."

"I think I know how you feel."

"Robert, when you move back home; are you going to stay here with your folks or get an apartment."

"I have no plans to move back. I was hoping after the divorce we could get together in California. We could bring your kids out and maybe even have one of our own."

"Divorce?"

"Yah, you said that you were going to get a divorce."

"I said that we were kind of separated. I never mentioned divorce. If I split with Dan, he would never forgive me and maybe even take the kids away from me. I know that he would never allow me to take them to

California. I thought you could get an apartment out here and we could meet two or three days a week. Wouldn't that be enough for you?"

"No! It's not enough. I love you and I always have. You said you loved me also.

"I do Robert, but I love my children more. I'm sorry if you are hurt."

"No, I'm ok. I guess I'm better off than if I hadn't seen you."

"So, Robert? We're in the orchard. Does that suggest something to you?"

"Fruit?"

"Come on Robert. We shouldn't let all this spoil a wonderful evening."

"Jessica, the evening is already spoiled, just like some of this fruit."

Robert kissed her very passionately then stood up. When she stood up, he took the blanket. Then turned toward the hole in the fence and said, "Goodnight".

"Robert, someday you will look back on this and remember it as a terrible mistake."

"I already do Jessica. Goodbye."

The next morning, Robert got out of bed and told Eric that he was the only person who knew where Robert lived, so if Jessica called, he was not to tell her anything. Just play dumb.

"That comes easy to me Bro."

"Eric what are you doing today?"

"I got a class at two."

"Can you take me to the Airport?"

"Sure. You wanna' watch the airplanes?"

"No, I'm going to Colorado."

"What is over there."

"Mom's daughter."

"Mom doesn't have a daughter. Just us three guys. I think I would have seen a girl walkin' around here."

"It was before you were born. Ask mom."

"When do you wanna' go?"

"Right after I say goodbye to mom."

His mother came out of the bedroom, followed by his father.

"You little son of a bitch." Said Earl.

"You should know."

"I don't ever want you in this house again."

"You aren't hurting my feelings ... Earl."

"You call me Mr. English."

"Funny that's my name ... until I have it legally changed."

"Get the fuck out of my house."

"But ... why are you going Robert?"

"Are you kidding me mom?" Robert asked shaking his head. "I'll talk to you later mom."

"Not on my telephone. You little asshole."

"Airport?"

"Thanks Eric. Are you and mom going to be ok?"

"Yah ... if he gives a bad time, I'll squash him like a pea."

They talked on the way to the airport, however he didn't tell his little brother about their dad being a child molester. Eric again helped him with his bags into the terminal. Robert told Eric, to tell Jim what happened. They boys gave each other a hug then Eric left to go to school.

Chapter 5

It was eleven o'clock in the morning, and Robert was on the third shuttle to Denver. The flight was only three hours, but as they were heading west it would be only about forty-five minutes on his watch, due to the time change. Robert was nervous from the time he sat down and buckled in.

The 737 revved up the engines, then taxied out on to the tarmac. The flight attendants went through the safety procedures and explained how everything worked. Suddenly although Robert wasn't ready, the airplane started down the runway and lifted into the air.

"Well here goes nothing." Said Robert as the little airplane broke through the clouds. Making a wide sweeping turn to head west. At Robert's request, the flight attendant brought him a double Jack Daniels on the rocks, which he drank down immediately, then ordered another.

After downing two doubles, Robert began to relax, and sat back to try and enjoy the flight. When he looked around at the other passengers, they all looked like terrorists, but he was a little higher than the airplane, so he just giggled.

What seemed to be about two or three minutes later one of the flight attendants was shaking his arm and telling him that they were now on the glide path into Denver International, and they would be landing in fifteen minutes. Robert took a chance and looked out the window. Although he expected a lot of trees and snow, the city was very desolate looking and there were no trees in sight.

When they landed it felt like all the tires were flat, but the plane taxied to the terminal, and some of the passengers began to get off. Robert was never so happy just to be on the ground. When the flight attendant said,

"Welcome to Denver and join us again."

Robert mumbled under his breath,

"Oh, yah like that will ever happen."

Robert picked up his bags and went over to the Hertz Rental agency, where he rented a little dark blue sedan. He also obtained a local, and state map and went to the car.

It was almost two o'clock, when Robert pulled the rental car up to "Our Lady of Sacred Love Academy and St. James High School" on Barton Street. He got out of the car and walked up to the school. He thought to himself he could just talk to her. If she liked the life she was living, he would leave.

As he entered the front door, he saw a sign, which displayed, Principal Leo Bonarotti. A very prim and proper secretary, in her late forties, with a very large nose, greeted him as though she had a mouth full of cotton. She picked her words carefully and said slowly, "May I help you sir?" and even though she said it, Robert knew by her attitude that she didn't mean it.

"I believe my sister is a nun here. I would like to speak with her."

"Her name?"

"Kathryn English."

"Sorry, she is allowed no visitors. Goodbye Sir." The woman turned her back on him and began shuffling some papers.

A Nun's Tale

"What the hell are you talking about?"

"I will have to ask you not to raise you voice, and refrain from using profanity. This is a Catholic School." She said still with her back toward him.

Robert reached over the desk, grabbed her chair and spun her around. She had an expression of someone riding a "tilt a whirl" at an amusement park.

"Listen very carefully ... lady." said Robert, "I don't care if this is the fucking Vatican. I said I want to talk to my sister."

The robot-like woman slowly lifted her arm and flipped a switch on an old maple- wood intercom box.

A voice answered. "Yes Miss. Murray, what is it."

"Mr. Bonarotti, there is a ... man ... out here who wishes to visit a nun," she said in a monotone voice. "Sister Mary Stewart. He refuses to take no for an answer."

The door to the Principal's office opened and a rather large man of about three hundred pounds with a bright red face, wiping perspiration from his forehead stared at Robert incredulously. It was obvious he was of Italian ancestry, as he looked more like more like a "Mafia" good guy than a schoolteacher. He said. "Please come in."

"My name is Robert English, and my sister Kathryn is employed here as a nun. I would like to speak with her."

"Didn't my secretary explain that it was not possible."

"There were words to that effect. But I don't accept her statement."

"Well what is it that you don't understand? This is a cloistered nunnery, and the sisters never speak to anyone."

"Why ... is she under arrest?"

"Of course not. She is here of her own free will. Do you not understand what a cloistered nunnery is?"

"Yes ... I'm Catholic. It means, separated from, and having little contact with the outside world."

"Well?"

"Little contact doesn't mean no contact at all, does it?"

"I'm awfully sorry, however those are our rules."

"May I ask how many nuns and priests are employed here?

"About fifty nuns, many of whom are teachers and twenty priests."

"Fine, I'll just give you my card. I work for a large western newspaper in California. Can you tell me the direction of the Sheriff's Department? I'm beginning an investigation in this area regarding priests who have been molesting children."

Bonaritti, sat motionlessly his face turning a deathly white, as though the blood bank had taken a little too much at his last donation.

"What is it that you really want Mr. English?"

"I really want to speak with my sister. Will you arrange that now?"

Bonaritti picked up the phone and entered three numbers on the pad.

A Nun's Tale

"Yes Miss. Swarthing, this is Bonaritti. I wish to speak to the Mother Superior."

"Reverend mother, I have a situation. We have a man who must speak with his sister, Mary Stewart ... Yes, I know that, however this is an emergency ... we will just have to forget the rules this one time ...Yes I will explain it to you later. OK that will be fine ... Yes OK."

The Principal hung up the phone and directed Robert down the hall to a recreation room. He took Robert in and had him sit in a chair in the middle of the room. There, he was left alone for about ten minutes, until one of the back doors opened and two nuns walked in. Robert stood as they walked over to him. It almost looked like a prison matron with and inmate.

They both appeared to be just over five foot, and they were dressed in heavy robes.

"Are you Kathryn English?" asked Robert.

The nun made no statement however nodded her head looking toward the floor. The other sister who was easily in her sixties, stood close to the younger one, holding her arm.

"Excuse me, but I would like to talk my sister alone."

"That is not possible."

"You wouldn't want to bet your rosary beads on it, would you Sister?"

"Well I was told ..."

"I know exactly what you were told," said Robert. "Now I'm telling you, if you want to keep this school out of the newspapers, off of television and out of the courts, you will leave this room immediately."

She stood looking at him, with a forty-year history of Catholic School behind her. She had handled many students in her time and Robert was no different.

"Did you not understand what I said sister?" Said Robert looking down into her eyes, not blinking about three inches from her face. "If things don't go my way and you people don't cooperate, I'll get this school closed down, no matter what it takes."

The little old nun, who resembling a thoroughbred pit bull, almost snared at him curling her upper lip, then turned and defiantly walked from the room.

He sat down next to the younger nun and asked,

"Do you know who I am Sister?

She shook her head however said nothing.

"I'm your brother Robert."

"Robert?" She had the beginning of a smile on her face, and tears welling up in her eyes.

"Yes. Robert English."

"Your mother is Marge and your Dad is Earl."

When Robert said Earl, she winced as though she were in pain."

"Do you remember Earl?"

"Yes. He told me not to tell."

"Tell what?"

"Not to tell?" She lowered her eyes to her hands folded together in her lap.

"What did he do to you? You can tell me, I'm your brother."

"Do ... you ... like ... Earl?"

"He's my father, but I don't like him. I don't believe anyone really likes him. What did he do to you?"

"He made me stay in the basement, in a chair."

"He tied you up, didn't he?"

"Yes!"

"I knew it!" Robert almost shouted out. "Then he touched you, didn't he?"

She began to cry and nodded her head.

"Earl said that he would hurt momma and me if I didn't let him touch me. Is momma alright?"

"Yes, momma is fine."

"Earl and momma had a fight and he said that I had to leave. I was brought here."

"Do you like it here?"

She looked all around to see if anyone could hear her and then whispered,

"No, they make me stay in my room and pray all of the time, and they hit me if I do anything wrong."

"What did you do that they thought was wrong?"

"I touched myself in my room."

"Do you mean, that you touch yourself ... down there."

She looked down embarrassed; a single tear flowed down her cheek.

"Do you want to stay here?"

"I have to ... they said ... I have to."

"No you don't. You don't have to stay, if you don't want to."

"I don't want to go back with Earl."

"No; of course not. You will never have to see Earl again."

"Where would I go Robert?"

"To California with me. With your little brother."

When she smiled his heart jumped. He had never seen such a smile on anybody before. She threw her arms around Robert and kissed him on the cheek. The tears were now flowing down her face and she said,

"Robert I'm so happy. You saved me."

Just then the older nun walked back in and told Robert that Sister Mary Stewart had to return to her cell.

"'Fraid not sis." He said showing no respect. "She is going with me."

"Are you insane young man? She isn't going anywhere."

"What would you say sister if I told you that there were several priests working here that have molested little boys, and quite a few nuns, who pass themselves as teachers, but constantly beat the children who live here."

"I wouldn't believe you."

"Do you want names?" asked Robert. "Bring her personal effects here now. We are leaving."

"Nuns have no personal effects." She said scornfully.

"Better yet." Laughed Robert. "Come on Kathryn we're going, and sister if you call the police and attempt to stop us. All of your dirty little secrets will be in the newspaper and on nationwide television tomorrow."

The older sister shook her head and said, "You know that you will go to hell for this."

"If I do, I'll be the one sitting on the hot coals right next to you."

The sister said nothing more, turned on her heals and left the room.

"This way Kathryn, I have a car outside."

They walked out to the lobby of the school, with Kathryn holding Robert's arm like they could take her back if she let go. As they approached the main door the Principal stepped in front of them. Kathryn stopped and waited for a moment.

"Come on sweetie, we have a train to catch."

"You are going to be sorry for this young man."

"Listen close asshole, if you fuckers don't leave us alone or say anything to anyone, I'll have the Vatican down on your ass. Not to mention the FBI. She never wanted to be here, and you have held her against her will for years. That's False Imprisonment for sure, and I might even be able to prove kidnapping. Ask Mother Superior what she would think spending twenty-five to life, in the Federal lock up, not that it would be much different than here. Do you still want to stand in our way?"

The Principal frowned then turned to go into his office. Robert and Kathryn walked out the front door and got into the car. She began to laugh and cry at the same time.

"What are you laughing about sister?"

"Please Robert don't call me sister anymore."

"Not their sister." Said Robert flipping his head toward the school. "My sister, sweetie."

She smiled and then laughed out loud. Her laughter was heady almost like hearing; perfume, and he was determined to make every effort, to make her laugh every day.

"What about clothes? I can't wear this robe all of the time, especially in California."

"What do you have on under your robe?"

"A bra."

"And panties?"

"No, they didn't give us any panties."

"You're kidding?"

"No."

"Do you know what size you are?"

"No. I'm sorry."

"Don't say you are sorry. You have nothing for which to apologize."

Then she lifted her robe and showed her brother that she was naked underneath.

"Does this help? What size do you think I am?"

Robert sat there staring into her lap. Her pussy mound was bare. The situation reminded him of some of his dates with Jennifer at the drive in.

"A ... a ... five ... maybe?" he stammered as he pulled away from the school and drove several blocks to the downtown area where he spotted a mall. Robert pulled into the mall and parked near a Mervyns store.

Inside the store everybody was looking at Kathryn in her robe and sandals. Robert pointed her toward the changing room and looked around for a panty display. He grabbed a white silky pair of lacy panties, size five and went in behind her. He was startled, as she was standing there completely naked.

"Sweetie, you shouldn't have taken off your robe until I left."

"Why? You are my brother."

"Yes, but brothers and sisters shouldn't see each other naked."

"Why not? In the book of Genesis, it said Adam and Eve had two sons and three daughters. His brother Kane killed the other son, Able. If there were no other people in the world, the remaining son must have had sex with his sisters, right?"

"I think that you have given this too much thought Katie ... Can I call you Katie?"

"Of course, you can Robert. In the nunnery they told us not to think, just pray; but sometimes I just had to think."

She turned to step into her panties, when Robert saw some scars on her back. He asked her where they came from, and she told him that many of the younger girls were beaten if they were caught touching themselves inappropriately.

It happened years ago and doesn't hurt anymore. Robert was furious but held it back. He wanted to return to the school and destroy everyone who had ever hurt his sister.

"What do you think Robert? She asked, smiling standing there in just a pair of white lace hip hugger panties. They were a perfect fit. Although she was older, she looked like she was no more than nineteen. Her perky breasts pointed at him as though they wanted to tell him something. She was so gorgeous he was having a hard time formulating words.

"Ga ... go ... good. They look good on you."

"Thank you. I like them ... very much."

Robert was getting a little excited when he asked her what her bra size was. She didn't know, but stood up straight and thrust out her breasts, then handed him the convent bra, which wasn't much help either.

He could see however from many years of looking at the female form, she was at least a "C" cup. He went back out into the store and located a salesgirl, telling her Katie's location and what he thought she needed.

A half hour later Katie came out looking like something out of a Magazine. She sure didn't look like a thirty-four year old woman. Her hair had been cut short to wear under the habit and looked very cute with her new clothes. She seemed truly happy and her blue eyes sparkled when she smiled.

"Robert, you have made me feel like a ... girl again. I love you."

"I love you too baby."

"Oh Robert, please don't call me baby. That's what Earl always called me."

"I'm so sorry."

"Thank you for understanding Robert."

Robert handed the salesgirl his Visa gold card and she rang up the bill. He watched Katie as she did pirouettes in front of a full-length mirror giggling. She had never had a life, and he was going to do his best to make a nice one for her.

With all of their packages in hand they went out to the rental car and moved over to a Savon Drug store. When they went in, Robert began to pick out things like toothbrushes, toothpaste, a comb and a brush, soaps and perfumes. Robert took her over to the feminine care products and asked her when her last period had come. She looked at him strangely and said,

"Period?"

"When you bleed down there," he said embarrassed and whispering, wishing he hadn't had to ask her.

"Oh that," she said brightly, "It was about a week ago, so maybe in two or three weeks," she said shrugging her shoulders.

Robert pointed to the feminine products lining the wall and asked what type of things they used. She told him that they had a room with a lot of buckets at the nunnery. Inside the buckets were large wads of cotton. When they were done, they flushed them down the toilet and scrubbed out the buckets.

Middle ages he thought. It wasn't going to be easy to bring her into the 21st Century.

"Which do you think will meet your needs sweetie?"

She reached up and pulled a large box of Kotex "maxi pads" from the shelf and handed them to Robert, and then they continued on to different sections of the store. Robert paid for everything and after they returned to the car, they headed North on I-25, stopped for gas, and then moved across the state boarder into Wyoming moving west on I-80.

They were headed toward Salt Lake City to board the train for San Francisco where Robert had left his car. Robert told Katie to lie down and take a nap if she wanted. She told him she hadn't been away from the school in years, and she just wanted to see everything.

She then moved closer to Robert an inch at a time, until she was next to him, resting against him. He smiled at her when she looked up at him. It felt strange, he thought. He was the younger brother by almost five years, yet he was taller and of course stronger and more knowledgeable of life.

She was tiny, not much more than five feet three inches, and she actually looked like she was just a kid. It was almost like she had been in a time capsule.

She remained quiet for a long stretch, until they were well onto the I-80 heading west. She moved her arm and looped it through his and said,

"Thank you, Robert ... thank you for everything."

"Your welcome Kitten."

"Is that my name ... to you? Kitten?"

"Kitten is an endearment and part of Kathryn, or Katie."

"I like it when you call me Kitten. It's nice."

"Kitten it is then."

She moved in closer and put her arms around him, as though she would awaken in her dark gray cell at any minute. As he drove the almost five hundred miles to Salt Lake, she fell asleep, however still hung onto him for dear life.

It was going to take them at least seven hours to get to Salt Lake City, and he would have to stop for dinner and more fuel. He knew that the whole time they had been together she hadn't eaten anything.

"Kitten, are you hungry?"

"They only let us eat once at noon, and a little energy bar in the evening with fruit and soup. They do give us a lot of water though. They told us hunger was good for us as it would make us feel like Jesus did when he fasted."

Robert had never remembered wanting to kill before this moment, and fought a desire to turn the car around, buy a gun and shoot everyone in the school. Columbine, he thought. Probably a bad idea; those damned assholes.

However, that was it. He now knew he was going to quit the church. Katie fell asleep, and then awakened an hour later when Robert pulled into a Restaurant.

"Robert?" she cried out holding him tighter.

"It's OK sweetheart. Everything is OK."

She sighed and really relaxed for the first time since they had started out. She was so beautiful. She was even more beautiful than Jennifer in many ways. The restaurant had no name, just a large sign that displayed the word, "EAT".

They went in and Robert showed her how to look at the food on the menu. She was surprised that she could have anything she wanted. It was almost like she was from a far-off planet in another solar system.

He watched her as she ate. Her table manners were impeccable; however she finished every crumb on her plate.

"Would you like something else? You can order anything you want."

"No thank you. I haven't eaten this much in a long time, and I am full. The food was very good."

"How about a piece of Apple pie, like mom used to make? If you can't eat it all, I'll share it with you."

"Apple pie?" she smiled. Robert waived at the waitress, and said,

"Two apple pies and two large glasses of milk."

"OK sport you got it."

A Nun's Tale

When Katie took her first mouthful of the pie, she said,

"Mmmmmm this is wonderful." She finished every crumb and every drop of milk.

If she believed this was good, thought Robert, wait until he took her to a five-star restaurant. It was now almost six in the afternoon and it was dark. The Chicago Zephyr was scheduled to stop in Salt Lake at four on the morning.

There was no point in trying to make the next morning's train. It had been a rough day for both of them and due to the "jet lag" it was nine o'clock for him. Paying the check, Robert asked the clerk if there was a good motel around.

The clerk, who appeared to be deriving some sustenance out of a toothpick, which he had been sucking on, made a fist and stuck his thumb over his shoulder.

"About how far?" asked Robert.

He looked at Robert as though he had been interrupted while contemplating a cure for heart disease. The man said,

"Four ... miles."

"Thanks."

Robert and his sister went to the car and he drove the four miles to a "Best Western Motel". It looked fairly nice, so he walked into the office, with Katie holding his hand tight.

A female of about thirty-five with coke bottle glasses was in the back room watching television, and when Robert taped the bell, she came sauntering out. She said nothing, however raised her eyebrows in a minimalist's way of asking what they wanted.

"A room?"

"We only got one, with a queen bed."

"Don't you have a room with two beds?"

"We only got one, with a queen bed."

Robert looked at his sister and said,

"They only got one with a queen bed." Mocking the woman.

Katie just smiled, raised her eyebrows and imperceptibly nodded her head.

The woman had a plastic badge that read Assistant Manager "MARGE". Robert almost stated that his mother's name was also Marge, but then thought better of it.

Forty-nine ninety-nine, including tax," she said and gave Robert the key. As the room was only two doors down from the office, they walked down the covered walk way. Robert opened the room and Katie peeked inside, but hesitated to go all the way in.

"What's wrong Kitten?"

"I was just looking to see who was here."

"Nobody is here. This is our room."

"Just for us?"

Robert nodded his head and brought in all the packages from the backseat of the car. However, left the other packages in the trunk.

It was dark outside, so automatically without thinking, Robert used the remote to turn the TV on. Katie sat on the end of the bed and, after Robert showed her how to use the remote, she remained there going through the channels, watching each for about five seconds, and then moving on to the next.

"Katie, I'm tired so I'm going to bed," he said, the effects of Jet lag beginning to atrophy his brain. "I don't have any pajamas so I will have to sleep in my briefs. I hope you don't mind."

"That is fine Robert." She said not turning her head away from the changing channels.

"Which side do you want?"

"I don't need a whole side Robert; I will just cuddle up with you."

"OK do you know where your pajamas are?"

"I didn't buy any Robert. The girl said that I should get some nighties and frilly things for you."

"Not for me, she meant for your boyfriend."

"She said they were for you."

Chapter 6

"We can talk about it tomorrow. I'm sorry but I'm going to bed."

He crawled in between the cool covers and fell asleep almost immediately. He felt her as she came to bed and crawled very close to him a little later. But then he was asleep again. Robert awoke to the bed shaking thinking that what he felt was an earthquake.

He looked at Katie who had her back to him, and a hand between her legs rubbing herself violently. It didn't take very long until she was groaning, and then suddenly she was relaxed again.

When she fell asleep, he began to drift off. He awoke at one in the morning. She was doing it again. He placed his arms around her as she continued to masturbate wildly. When she finally came, she turned around and hid her face in his shoulder and cried, hugging him hard.

"I'm sorry Robert," she sobbed, "Sometimes I just need it so bad; I can't stand it."

"It's OK Kitten, sometimes I need it too."

"Honest Robert? You need S-E-X?" she asked, spelling it out, "as much as I ... do?"

"Of course, Kitten. There are times that I have to play with my penis, to relieve myself just like you were doing."

She got much closer, reached around him and pulled him as close as she could. When she pushed her belly against him, he was unable to control himself and began to get hard. He knew that there were rules against what he was thinking, so he moved back just a little, hoping she hadn't felt it, but it was too late,

"Robert was that your pee-pee poking me?"

"Yes ... I'm sorry."

"Don't be sorry. I like the feeling. It was nice."

"You had better go to sleep, my sexy little sister, before I ..."

"... before you what Robert?"

"Before I spank you bottom for being a naughty girl."

"I'm not naughty Robert. I'm just interested. I have never been in bed with a man before. It's really nice. I like the feel of your body against me."

"Go to sleep, we have almost eight hours of driving tomorrow."

"Why?"

"Well we want to get into Salt Lake to catch the train."

"But you said that the train departs at four in the morning. Wouldn't it be better to get there around midnight so we wouldn't have to wait so long?"

"I guess ... but I don't have our tickets yet and I have to turn in the car."

"You should call the car rental and ask where you can turn it in late, near the station, then call the station and make reservations for us on the train."

Robert was pleased that she knew a little bit about the outside world and used her logic. He squeezed her hard and gave her a kiss on her forehead. She in turn grabbed hold of his face and pulled his lips down to her. She kissed him long and soft, finally sucking on his lower lip. Robert was a little excited and shoved his tongue into her sweet mouth, touching her tongue.

They continued this action for about a half hour, until he was on his back, and she was lying on top of him, her legs on both sides of him and her crotch rubbing on his swollen cock.

"Your pee-pee feels so nice rubbing me down there Robert."

Robert remembered that she was his half-sister, and they shouldn't be doing this.

"Kitten maybe we should stop, before we go too far. Go to sleep and we can talk about it in the morning."

"Robert," she said, crawling off of him, "I'm so excited now. I have to relieve myself again."

As she lay on her left side, with him close behind her, she slid her hand into her panties and began to rub.

"If you want, I will help you Kitten."

"How", she asked looking at him over her shoulder. Robert reached under the covers took hold of her panties and pulled them down and off her feet. He then removed his jockey shorts and got close to her.

"Only if you want to have children."

"I have never wanted to have children, Robert. Are we going to make love now?

"Are sure you really want to?"

"Oh yes. Jenny told me that it was the most wonder feeling in the world, and I want to do it with you. Would you mind doing it with your sister?"

"No... Not if it's what you want."

"I really want to Robert ... with you."

Robert wanted to treat her special, so he held her close for a long while, and kissed her tenderly. Moving down to her neck, he sucked long but not hard so as not to leave marks. She was responding to him with her whole body now.

He kept moving down kissing her just above her breasts, which were turning a bright pink; he then turned his attention to her nipples that stood up like little pencil erasers. He could feel that she was at the height of her excitement, due to the impulsive and uncontrolled movements of her body, so very slowly he knelt between her thighs.

She surprised him when her legs, hooked around his and attempted to pull him in. She was in fact very ready to take the next step, and who better to do it with, than her own brother, who loved her more than he ever knew he could.

He held his cock and gently slid the head up and down her slit touching her vaginal opening, then returning back to her clitoris, and back down again. Robert could feel he was making progress when he felt her short nails scraping his back. He was happy that the convent had made the nuns keep their nails short.

Knowing that his sister had never had a man before, he wanted her first time to be special, and slowly pushed his swollen cock into the slippery entrance of her vagina. She moaned and groaned, as the feeling to her was beyond anything she had ever experienced. She was no longer a child of God. With Robert's help she had become a child of lust. She loved the feeling he was giving her and would do anything to make him feel wonderful too.

Taking a long time Robert eased his penis into her pussy. It took almost forty minutes to push it in all of the way. He felt bad when her broke her cherry, because of the extreme pain it caused her, but she never complained holding him tight the whole time.

All she did to ease the pain was bite her lower lip. When his cock was finally in her all the way, she looked in his eyes and smiled, then nodded her head letting him know she was ready for him to do it to her.

As her pussy was so tight, Robert began very slowly which caused an almost intolerable feeling of a craving and desire for both of them.

"Please Robert." She said.

"What Kitten?"

"Please do it to me a little faster. It won't hurt me honest. I love your pee-pee in me. You are the part of me that has been missing for so long. Do it faster ... please."

He pulled his cock out almost all the way out which caused an audible sucking sound. When she thought he was going to remove his penis, she moved her hips up fast attempting to keep it inside of her. She was pleasantly surprised when he shoved back into her, meeting her upward thrust with great force.

It was a little painful, but wonderful as he caused her to cum again. She was thirty-four and at the height of her sexual peek. Robert was now wondering if he would require mechanical assistance to keep her satisfied.

He decided to go for broke and really "put it to her" as the saying goes. He doubled his efforts and jammed it deep into her as hard as he could. She was beyond excited and cuming every few minutes. She now was where she was supposed to be and loved every second of it.

To her being a sex partner was much more important than being a nun. Oh my, she thought, he was making her squirt again. He was wonderful, and she loved him more than just a half-brother. If this were the way it would always be, she would never have to touch herself again.

He was fantastic, and he knew about everything she needed. Now she had to find out everything her little brother needed. He made her cum again, and then he squirted in her. When he rolled off of her, she crawled into his arms and told him what a wonderful brother; and lover he was.

He made her so happy she didn't know how to tell him. She would be his as long as he wanted. Soon as they were both satisfied, they fell asleep. The next morning, they awoke at six thirty, and she reached down and fondled his cock.

"Do you like my cock?" he asked.

"Cock? Is that what you call it. I like the name. Can I call it a cock too?"

"Sure, you can. Cock or Penis."

"What do you call my pee-pee slit Robert?"

"A pussy, or a vagina and when I'm really excited maybe a cunt?"

"Yes?"

"Mr. Cock, meets miss. Pussy." She then laughed and began stroking Robert's penis.

"Robert touch my pussy and make it wet. Then we can do what we did last night. I liked that a lot."

"You want to fuck again, this morning. Aren't you hungry?"

"Not right now. We can eat later ... can't we? She asked smiling biting her lower lip."

"We can do anything you want baby, anytime that you want."

She then flopped on her back, spread her legs and opened her arms.

"No," said Robert, "It's your turn on top. I want you to sit on my lap."

Katie looked at him in a strange way. She had never heard of such a thing, but if that's what he wanted, she wasn't going to say no. She knelt next to him for a few seconds not sure what to do.

Her cute little baby dolls were complementing her tiny shape. He showed her what to do, and how to swing her leg over him. When she did, her pussy became a target for his cock, and although it was tight, it slid in with little trouble. When she felt his cock buried inside of her, she was complete again.

Katie looked at him, for a minute smiling, however, didn't know the next move.

"Robert I'm not sure what to do. Do I jump up and down or what?"

"Move a little forward Kitten and then back. Do whatever feels good to you."

"Everything feels good to me. Everything you do." She moved a little forward, not really knowing what to expect. After only a few moves and seconds later, she was in sexual heaven rocking, front to back, a little harder each time, her hands on his chest.

Within minutes Robert was fascinated that his sister, the ex-nun was sitting on his cock and moving as fast as any girl he had ever know. She loved everything about sex and constantly asked questions about everything. She slowly began moving forward, feeling the telltale signs of an impending orgasm.

When she lay down on his chest, he thrust up into her vagina hard, causing her to squeal an ear-piercing sound that made all the dogs within a half-mile set up and cock their ears. Luckily the sound she made was almost inaudible to the human ear.

Although Robert wasn't really horny when she began, he was now getting into it, and enjoying her extravagant act very much. She was naturally sexy and enjoyed everything they did together. He wondered if she would ever suck him. That would come in the future, as there was no rush. After all they had only really known each other less than twenty-four hours.

Robert began to feel like he was going to cum when she had her third orgasm. He placed his arms around her, fucking as hard as he could driving his cock up into her vagina. She sat up a little and looked straight into his eyes. She had an expression as though something was not right. Like it wasn't what she was expecting somehow.

Seconds later her pussy shouts out a thick creamy discharge; all over her little brother's cock and testicles. Her involuntary action triggered Robert to begin cuming on his own mixing his juice with hers, and she could almost feel her cervix sucking his sperm in to her.

This was way beyond anything she had ever hoped would occur. Now she understood why God had given her all the equipment for sex, he wanted her to use it and be happy, and make somebody else happy also.

Although she had slept well and hadn't got out of bed yet, she lay down on her brother's chest, breathing hard, his stiff cock still imbedded inside of her. She always knew all those years, while she prayed constantly for guidance, that there was something missing.

She had attempted to fill her need for something by pleasuring herself, two or three times a day, but it never came close to what she and Robert had been doing with each other. She had reached an epiphany and now knew the real purpose of life. It had nothing to do with praying for world peace, it was making someone you loved happy, and enjoying what they had to offer in return. She believed that if everyone would do that, there would in fact, be world peace.

Exhausted, she crawled into her little brother's arms cuddling as close to him as possible. He was warm and a little wet where her perspiration had dripped down on him.

They awoke again at eight-forty-five and although she had given Robert her let's do it smile, he told her that they were going to take a shower, and then go to breakfast. He wanted to cover at least five hundred miles today. He called the "Hertz" rental company and had found out that he could drop the car at the train station twenty-four hours a day.

When they got out of bed, she looked at him like a little girl who had been told that she had been grounded for being naughty. When he asked her what was wrong, she said,

"Nothing Robert," then looked down at the floor biting her lower lip.

He knew right away what was going on.

"Sweetie, there is more to life than just sex."

"You can say that, because you have been doing it for years. I just found about it yesterday."

"But if you do it too much, you'll get bored with it, and won't want to do it anymore."

"Never Robert. I'll never get bored doing it with you."

"Come on Kitten, let's take a shower."

"Together? Is that ok?"

"Of course, it is, besides it saves water and we can wash each other's backs."

As he was already naked, she stood there looking at his wonderful penis, just wishing ... and breathing hard.

He turned on the water, then pulled her baby dolls over her head and gently pulled her into the shower. He unwrapped the bar of motel soap and began to lather his hands. When he placed them on her full tender breasts she moaned, thinking that this was wonderful torture.

As Robert washed his sister's titties, her nipples stood up showing that she was in the mood. Robert then moved down and washed her stomach, then moved down telling her to spread her legs. Washing her hairless mound and slit, she groaned with the feeling of intense pleasure he was giving her.

He grabbed her shoulders and told her to turn around and bend over. He lathered up his hand and began washing between her butt cheeks. When he slid a finger into her rectum, to clean it, she knew that there was more to come. He slid a soapy finger into vagina, and then quickly rinsed it. She knew that this was the only way she would ever take a shower from that time on.

As she was bent over, Robert got behind her and slid his cock into her vagina. All she could think of was, 'Oh boy, oh boy, oh boy'. Holding her hips, he thrust forward and began to fuck her again. This was going to be the best shower she ever had. Her pussy was squeezing him and milking him to get the most out of what they were doing; with the warm water beating down on them adding an extra level to their love making.

After the second time she came, she almost fell over, so he turned her around and sat her down on a little shower seat. She sat there taking great pleasure and delight in what he had just done for her, wondering why his penis was still hard.

"Why are you still hard?"

"You looked a little tired, and I wasn't ready to cum yet. It's ok."

She took the soap from him and washed his testicles, then moved on to his penis. She spent a long time washing, caressing and fondling it. She rinsed it off and then asked,

"What can I do for you? How can I make it special, like you make it for me?"

"Would you like to kiss it a little?"

"Do girls do that?"

"Yes, a lot of girls do. Some of them even take the whole thing in their mouth and suck on it until it squirts. Then they swallow the guy's cream."

"Really? It doesn't hurt them?"

"No. It's just like when I suck you between your legs. You said you liked that."

"Oh yes. That is wonderful. Do you want me to do it to you?"

"Only if you really want to."

"I'm not sure I can do it like other women Robert." She was now sitting on the shower seat, with his cock not two inches from her face. It was long, hard and beautiful. She stuck her tongue out a little and touched the tip of his penis. It didn't taste bad and she knew it was clean, as she had just washed it.

Taking just the tip of his long penis in her mouth, her natural instincts took over and she sucked a little. Katie then moved her face foreword a little more and took the whole head into her mouth. She sat there for a moment, unsure of what to do until she heard Robert say,

"Suck ... harder ... baby."

Katie started to suck just a bit more, until she decided it really tasted kind of good. It wasn't a foreign piece of something that shouldn't be there, as it filled her mouth and felt really nice. She knew that her brother would not intentionally hurt her so; she sucked a little harder and enjoyed the feeling of his penis in her mouth. After just a few minutes Katie felt her brother's hands on the back of her head holding it steady, as he moved his hips plunging deeper into her mouth.

Less than five minutes had passed when she tasted a sweet, bitter, salty liquid that had the consistency of raw egg whites but tasted just a little like ... she wasn't exactly sure. Then all of sudden there was a lot more of it. The stuff almost filled her mouth. She pulled her mouth off her brother's penis and looked up at him. After a deep sigh, he looked down at her and said,

"Swallow it sweetie."

When she did, she thought that it wasn't bad, and she would do it always to make him feel good. He then got down on the floor of the shower, spread her legs and moved his face in between them. When he began to suck, she was again in heaven. She came twice in the first few minutes, and once more several minutes later.

When they finally got out of the shower, he began to dry her with the rough motel towel leaving her skin a bright pink, and then he dried himself. They got dressed in silence, and walked out to the car, all of the packages in hand. Robert went into the office and dropped the key on the desk.

"Room 106," he said.

A clerk looked up at him and made a nod of his head. Robert turned and walked out the door.

They drove west then stopped for breakfast at a dinner. The food wasn't bad, but they ate and got out of there. After filling the tank across the street, they were on the road again. After several hours of driving they came to the little town of Rawlins Wyoming.

It was still almost three hundred miles to Salt Lake City. Robert told Katie that it might be a good idea to rest up overnight, and part of the next day, then leave around nine. That would put them in Salt Lake around two am, so they could drop off the car at the train station and would only have to wait two hours for the train.

Rawlins a little town sitting on the Continental Divide, was named after General John A. Rawlins, Chief of Staff of the U.S. Army, who after taking a drink from a spring in 1867, at the base of a nearby hill declared,

"If anything is ever named after me, I hope it will be this spring of water."

It was about one in the afternoon, when Robert found a motel, and got a room for two nights. It was a nice motel and best of all it had a heated indoor swimming pool. The weather had dropped into the low fifties, and he was pleased Katie had purchased some warm clothing, and a nice jacket. She looked so cute all bundled up, like a beautiful little Eskimo in her hooded parka.

There wasn't much to say about Rawlins, other than they had a Recreation Center the size of a small Balley's Spa, and the Sinclair Golf Course. During the summer months of June, July and August, they had Music in the Park staring all local musicians. In June there was Sierra Rose, and the next week there was Brenn Hill, ect, ect, ect.

The most famous fact about Rawlins, is the History of Big Nose George Parrot who was Rawlins' most famous outlaw. In 1878 he and an accomplice tried to rob a payroll train just east of Rawlins. The robbery was a failure, but they managed to elude capture, killing two of the pursuing posse.

When the law finally caught up with Parrot several years later, he was returned to Rawlins, tried and sentenced to hang. His attempt to break out of jail before his sentence was carried out shortened the process. A Rawlins mob lynched him. Up to this point, his story is fairly normal for Wyoming in the 1800's, but what happened next was a little bizarre.

Rawlins physician Dr. John E. Osborne took possession of the body, made a death mask of Parrot's famous profile, sawed open his skull to see how an outlaw's brains looked, and then presented the skull cap to his female assistant who used it for years as a door stop. Then Osborne skinned poor Parrot, tanned his hide as one might do with a cowhide, and made shoes and other items from the leather.

Finally, he pickled what was left of the body in a whiskey barrel. Actually, thought Robert the most interesting fact of all was that Dr. Osborne's macabre experiments had no noticeable impact on his public standing, as ten years later he was elected governor of Wyoming, and he later served as a senator. And people say that Californians' are weird.

Robert and Katie drove around town and found a movie theater, which was closed for renovations. So, they stopped at the Coffee shop and had some lunch. Afterward there was apparently nothing to do but return to the motel and take a nap or go swimming.

Katie voted for a nap, but Robert knew what she meant. Robert stopped by a local store and purchased a medium size suitcase and an overnight bag for Katie's new clothes. Then they went next door to a video rental store, whose owner seemed to care less that Robert was a California resident.

They rented one adventure story, one love story and two triple x-rated movies, and then headed back to the motel. Katie went into the bathroom and when she came out, she had on a pair of black panties that fit perfectly. She was also wearing one of Robert's white t-shirts. The combination made his cock hard almost immediately.

When she got on top of the King-sized bed, she looked so tiny that he was almost afraid to join her, but he slipped one of the DVD's in the machine and turned it on. When Katie saw what the couple was doing her eyes opened wide and she asked,

"Robert who are those people?"

"Porn actors."

"Actors? They do that for money?"

She was excited and giggling at the actions of the couple and told Robert that she was very happy that he got the movie, as now she could see what other people did in bed. As they laid back and watched the movie, she would ask questions each time something new occurred on the TV.

"What are they doing there Robert?"

"That is called "doggie style", because he is doing it to her from behind."

"What about that?"

"That is called sixty-nine as they are sucking each other at the same time."

"I think I would like to try that," she said unemotionally as if she were talking about picking out some new clothing.

"Oh," she said a little while later, seeing the girl giving the guy a blowjob, "I know what that is. She is sucking his cock ... Mmmm, she looks like she likes it."

Finally, after about fifteen minutes of watching the movie, Katie asked him if they could turn it off for a while so he could do it to her. He picked up the remote and shut everything off. Lying down next to her, he dropped his hand to her tummy and began to rub. He then moved it down to the crotch of her panties, and she spread her legs wide.

It only took a few minutes and her panties were damp. She whispered in his ear,

"Bobby take my panties off and put your big penis inside of me ... please.

As he didn't want to disappoint her, he slowly slid her panties down and off her feet. Quickly he removed his jockey shorts and knelt between her legs, with his hands on both sides of her head. Before he thought of taking hold of his cock, she had reached down and grabbed it with both of her tiny hands and guided it to the entrance of her vagina in an attempt to coat it with her natural juices.

Katie moved the head of his cock up and down her lips and clitoris, as Robert had done before. Her slippery labia coated his penis, making it easier to move into her vagina. She then moved it to the gateway of her lust and pulled hard to so that his cock would slide into her cunt. The feeling, which she was becoming more dependent upon for her satisfaction, was now much more wonderful than her past tortured dreams.

Chapter 7

Although she was aware society frowned on it, she truly loved this young man, her half-brother who, had saved her from a life of incarceration and boredom, then propelled her into a new life filled with love, lust and adventure. As his penis slid into her and his balls bumped into her sphincter, she knew that her life would no longer be dull.

Robert knew fully well what his sister needed, so as his cock was moving deep within her, he slid his hands under her butt cheeks and shoved his penis harder and harder, allowing it to come in contact with every centimeter of her mucus covered vagina.

After just a few strokes of his massive member she came, holding him tight against her letting him know he was needed more than ever, and she was begging him to continue.

Comparing this type of sex, to what he had with Jennifer was not easy, as they were two completely different women, with different needs and wants, desiring a similar gratification. All he could say was he loved fucking both of them, however his sister was more important to him now and in her own way offered him a lot more.

As his hard penis shoved relentlessly into his sister's pussy, he leaned his head down and sucked her titties, bringing her to the height of her sexuality. Then while still pounding his thick cock into her tender body, he kissed her lightly on the mouth, sucking on her lips and tongue.

She made a muffled groan as she again began to leak her thick fluids around Robert's penis. Although he was doing it to her, he had no desire to cum yet. His energy level was high, so he was going to continue fucking her until she begged him to stop. She came twice more in the next ten minutes then said,

"Robert ... do my breasts, like we saw them do in the movie. Stick your penis between my titties and squirt in my face. That looked like fun. I have never done it before."

"Neither have I, and I'm afraid my weight might hurt you."

"If it's uncomfortable, I'll tell you. Get on top of me and stick your penis between my titties and fuck them a little. When you squirt, try to get some of it in my mouth. It will be fun ... you'll see."

Robert gradually got on top of Katie, and gently laid his penis between her breasts. She squeezed them together tightly so he could fuck them. As he did, his body was rubbing against her nipples and she was getting hotter. The faster he moved, the further his cock went and several times it touched her mouth. When it did, she kissed it and tried to suck on the end.

He was now very excited, and he felt his cum, start to squirt. As it shot out the end of his penis, she opened her mouth wide and caught some of it, smiling. She then told him to push his penis in her mouth so she could finish sucking it.

"Mmmmmmmmm Robert, I think that I'm really beginning to like your stuff. It tastes so good."

Robert slid down her body, stopping to suck on her cute little breasts, knowing they soon would be increasing in size due to all of their activities. He then moved down kissing her tummy and then slowly down to her pussy. He was going to go for broke and give her so many orgasms that she would cry "uncle", actually cry "brother".

He kissed the top of her tight little slit, until her clitoris poked out to see what was going on. Licking it for a while Katie moaned and caressed his head with both hands, acknowledging the pleasure he was providing. She didn't pull his hair like Jennifer had; she just stroked his head, running her hands through his hair. It felt wonderful.

As Robert continued to kiss and suck, her pussy opened magically like a beautiful pink flower greeting the morning. Her flower was damp and had droplets of dew that he began to lick off. As he lifted her legs with both hands, she reached down and caught herself under her knees and pulled her legs back as far as they would go, presenting herself open wide to him.

The both held her legs as his mouth toured her vulnerable labia and vagina, sucking and licking every part of her beautiful cunt. As her vagina was wide open and begged to be lovingly assaulted, Robert slid his tongue into it as deep as he could pumping it in and out, causing her to cry out,

"Bob-bee, bob-bee, bob-bee, bob-bee, bob-bee, bob-bee, bob-bee, Oh ... Bobby."

As she sprayed his face with her orgasm, she dropped her legs unable to evoke the strength to hold them up any longer. He continued to suck her, and tongue fuck her until it seemed to deplete her store of multiple orgasms and she lay back quietly.

This was a special event however, and although she lay back with her eyes closed and her mouth hanging open, her arms flopped to her sides, Robert was going to try and push her over the edge. He was going to make her dream, of being violated to within an inch of her life, come true.

Her pussy was oozing her delicious liquid, and although he wanted to get down and lick up her flowing nectar, he moved up and slid his thick cock into her quivering and trembling cunt. She could no longer think, however her legs as though powered by some unknown force, hooked themselves around her brother's thighs and pulled him deep into her vagina.

He began to pump hard and knew he was reaching some invisible goal when she began to sob. He knew that he was not hurting her, as he had fucked her much harder before. He was aware she was just releasing her pent-up emotions and getting her body ready to have another orgasm.

Robert was surprised when her groin muscles began squeezing his cock. He couldn't understand where she learned this little-known sexual trick. She had it perfected however, as her vagina was sucking him hard. It was now becoming a contest to see who would make the other cum first.

Robert doubled his efforts and jammed his swollen penis inside of his sister's vagina moving very fast, the wetness almost overwhelming. Although he could feel his release, building in his back, thighs and balls, he was aware that she was ready also, buy the way her nails buried themselves in his butt.

A loud groan followed by a saturating gush of fluids, discharged from his sister's cunt. At the same exact time Robert began to cum also. This was a memorable occasion as it was the first time they had cum simultaneously. He laid on top of her, his cock remaining in her vagina, which was still pumping him and sucking his cock involuntarily. He felt she was quite satisfied, although her nails were still embedded in his ass cheeks.

Robert slowly lifted himself off of Katie, and then lay down beside her. The room was cool, so he pulled the bed cover over her almost naked body. As he stroked her short cut dirty blonde hair, she opened her eyes and smiled at him, her deep dimples indenting her bright pink cheeks.

"Thank ... you ... Bobby ... you are all that I need."

Katie then turned over and went to sleep. Robert suddenly felt a loss as his little sex partner had finally quit on him, but she hadn't done it without a fight. This situation was so far removed from Jennifer, and her family that it seemed like the whole Jennifer thing was just a distant memory.

He wondered what would have happened if Jennifer had agreed to go to California with him. What would have happened to his sister? Apparently, someone wanted him to see Katie and rescue her. It had to have been fate, as there was no other answer. At least there was no other answer that he could think of.

Robert slipped back into his underpants and put on a t-shirt. He took one of the DVDs out of its sleeve and placed it on the machine. The movie was called, "Serendipity" which meant a happy coincidence. He had seen the movie before, however had enjoyed it so much that he rented it, especially for Katie.

The movie stars; John Cusack and Kate Beckinsale. He is Johnathan and she is Sara. Jonathan and Sara meet when they reach for the same pair of black cashmere gloves in a crowded Manhattan department store five days before Christmas. After pleading their respective cases of who should rightfully get the gloves, Jonathan concedes and allows her to purchase them.

Sara buys him a coffee at a bakery called "Serendipity" to thank him, and the two hit it off, but as both are seeing other people, they don't become involved. Sara, who is a firm believer in fate, jots her name and telephone number down in a book and says she will sell it to a used bookstore the following day. If she and Jonathan are destined to be together, she rationalizes, the book will find its way to him.

Sara and Jonathan spend the following years thinking of each other, the memory of that magical night etched into their brains forever. Although he is about to be married, not to Sara however, he locates the book and a whirlwind search is launched for the love of his life. Through a bunch of "Serendipitous" mistakes they finally find each other.

Robert sat down and started the movie. For an hour and a half, he was lost in the abilities of the actors to, almost project him into another place.

He enjoyed the movie as much as the first time he saw it. Katie was beginning to stir and looked around to see if Robert was there. When she saw him, he waved and smiled. She smiled back contentedly.

"Are you hungry sweetie?" he asked. She said nothing, however smiled again and nodded her head.

"Ok ... why don't we get dressed and go out to get something to eat? If you go out dressed like that, your cute little rear end will probably freeze off."

Katie's smile turned into a giggle then she got out some new panties, a bra, a pair of long pants and a sweater. After they both were fully dressed, she walked up to Robert and stood in front of him.

"Robert, do you know how much I love you?"

"No!"

"You never will because it is more than the world and God himself."

"Little girl, I think that I may love you even more."

They left the motel and went looking for a nice restaurant. Robert saw a Chinese restaurant and asked her if she liked Chinese food. She shrugged her shoulders and said,

"I don't know. I have never had any."

"Would you like to try some?"

"Do you like it?"

"Oh yes. It can be wonderful."

A Nun's Tale

They went into the restaurant and sat in a booth. Robert pointed out all of the dishes he liked, and she told him to order for the two of them. Robert ordered two Mandarin dinners and two Pepsis. She was a little hesitant at first, but after tasting the food she ate it like he had never seen before. After dinner they went for a walk around the downtown area. She told him about her life and her twenty-five years in the convent and all of the girls she had met. He told her all about Santa Barbara and his apartment, his job and the things in which she had to look forward.

They got in the car and returned to the motel. She decided that she wanted to see the other triple x-rated movie. The second movie was similar to the first, except it was supposedly in Las Vegas. The actors were doing all the same stuff only in a slightly different order. After watching for fifteen minutes Katie began to get undressed, and when she was down to her birthday suite, she began to take off Roberts clothes. When they were both completely naked, she pulled the covers back, and they crawled in.

"Bobby get behind me and push your penis between my legs like you did the other night ... when you helped me the first time ... remember?"

He moved in behind her and she quickly lifted her leg over him then reached between her legs, took hold of his cock and laid it against her pussy lips. She then closed her leg, trapping him. As he began to move his hips she moaned and shoved her hips back. As his cock slid into her vagina, she pushed back helping him fuck her. Ten minutes later, she had him on his back and was sitting with her legs wide apart, astride him, his cock just where she wanted it, all the way into her pussy. She then began to move like a cat on steroids, undulating her hips and butt, as if she were sitting on a mechanical bull.

It didn't take very long until she stopped moving, moaned and squirted her juices. A mild orgasm didn't stop her however, and she continued to fuck her brother for all she was worth. This was now her vocation, keeping both herself and Robert satisfied. She loved fucking him, more than anything else. Robert thought maybe she would slow down in the future, and if not, what the hell he didn't want to live forever anyway.

When she came the second time, he moved down between her legs and put his mouth to work, licking and sucking. She quickly came again and told him in a whisper that he was extraordinary. As his face was very wet from her discharge, he began to move up her tummy, kissing and sucking all the way. When he came to her titties, she groaned as his mouth took in one of her nipples.

Robert sucked for a very long time and was a little surprised when she came just from his sucking. He then stuck an index finger into her butt hole and his thumb into her vagina. She came unglued and squirted again, knowing there was nothing short of death that would ever part them.

Pulling his fingers from her holes, he had her lay on her stomach, and shoved a pillow under her tummy. He then pushed her legs together as tight as he could then got on top of her and worked his cock into her pussy. She quickly grabbed another pillow and hung on for dear life. It was exquisite and felt like he was fucking her with an animal penis. He kept it up for almost an hour then came, filling her vagina with his cum and her discharge.

When she finally fell asleep, she didn't even bother to remove the pillow. The next morning, they both woke up around seven. She was exhausted and very happy. As they weren't hungry, they laid in bed watching movies. She however just couldn't keep her hands off of him and began to jack him off, as she had seen in the naughty movies. She stroked him for more than an hour until she became aware that he was about to cum. She slowly lowered her open mouth onto his penis and sucked hard, lightly squeezing his balls.

Then just like "Old Faithful" his stomach began to rumble and his cum filled her mouth. The flavor was exceptionally good, maybe because of the Chinese food the night before. It was noon before they dragged out of bed and went out to eat.

They both had a salad and a coke then returned to the motel. She thought that maybe this was what a real honeymoon might be like, but most honeymoons end. She made a promise to herself that this one never would. They made love in every way possible all afternoon, and then he called the office and left a call for nine o'clock, so they could get up and head for Salt Lake to catch the train.

Chapter 8

The telephone in the motel room began to ring in a muffled tone, and a red light started to flash. Robert lifted the receiver and a voice came on. "This is your nine o'clock wake up call."

Robert thanked the disembodied voice and hung up. Katie was still out, so Robert leaned over and kissed her. Her response was almost immediate. She put her arms around her brother and began to kiss him back with her eyes still closed. Her tongue slipped into his mouth and touched his.

"Robert ... kiss my titties, suck on them ... please."

He knew not to argue the point, so he placed his mouth on her nipple and began to suck. She in turn reached under the covers and took hold of his penis, stroking it slowly. When his cock began to get hard, she got on his lap and slipped his cock into her vagina. She then leaned forward and placed her nipple back into his mouth. Robert continued sucking while she moved front to back on top of him, her fluids beginning to flow.

Robert knew that they could leave the motel by eleven and be in Salt Lake before four am, but he really wanted to be out of there by ten. She was riding him for about forty minutes, and had two or three orgasms, however she apparently didn't want to stop, so Robert rolled her off and onto her stomach and got in behind her. He aimed as well as he could and shoved his cock into her damp little pussy. She flinched, and then moaned, as it felt wonderful to her.

He pulled on her pelvic bone and shoved harder and harder, penetrating her as deep as he could. Although she made no sounds, she would periodically gush out thick liquid, onto his penis helping everything to stay well lubricated. He knew at this point he was not about to cum so he would just continue for another half hour, hopefully until she was at least satisfied. When she "gushed" around the fifth time, she said,

"OK ... OK you win. I can't do this any longer, for a while anyway. You have burned me out."

"Are you ready to get up? I want to be out of here by ten."

"Ok Bobby, but I need a shower. Are you going to join me?"

"No ... you go ahead, and I'll take one after you."

"Ooooooo ... all right." She groaned as if somebody had taken away her favorite toy, and then went into the bathroom.

While his sister was in the shower, he packed everything he could, and laid out some clothes for the both of them. After she came out, he went in.

"Robert do you need anything washed ... I'm really good at that."

"No sweetie, just get dressed and I'll wash myself."

"OK," she sighed.

Just like clockwork, he thought. Everything went fine and they had departed the motel by ten, in route to San Francisco. The drive was tedious, especially at night, however Katie was awake and sitting as close to her brother as she could without actually sitting in his lap. She then asked,

"Robert when we catch the train, how long will it be to San Francisco?"

"About eighteen hours, why?"

"That's a long time to go ......"

"Without sex?" he finished her sentence.

"Well ... yah!"

"Sweetie, everything will work out. You will see."

"Still that's a long time."

Robert leaned over and kissed her on the top of her head, and continued driving. After two hours he pulled into a gas station and refueled. Katie just sat in the car, pouting.

As they left the gas station, she asked,

"Bobby ... do you think we can stop along the way ... and maybe ... do it in the car?"

"No sweetie. We don't want to take a chance on being caught by the police, now do we?"

"I guess not, but eighteen hours Bobby ... That's a long time."

"You'll live."

'Yah ... I guess."

"Concentrate on something else, like what you want to do when we arrive in San Francisco."

"That's easy. The same thing I want to do right now."

"Where is my jacket Kitten?"

"Are you cold Bobby?"

"No ... but I need my jacket."

Katie reached into the back seat and grabbed Roberts jacket, then looked at him with anticipation.

"Pull your panties down, sweetie."

"Huh?"

"Take your panties off and put them in your purse."

Not being one to argue, she lifted her dress hooked her thumbs in the top of her panties and pulled them down to her knees.

"All the way off sweetie."

She pulled them down and off her feet, then placed them in her purse as instructed. Robert then told her to get close to him and place his jacket on her lap. When she did that, he reached under her dress and began playing with her pussy.

After just five miles his middle finger was inside of her vagina and pumping her as fast as he could. This was heaven and much better than she could have done on her own. She moaned and began to cum, as his long finger continued to probe her depths.

"Oh Bobby ... you are so good to me. Do you think we can do this on the train?"

"I'm sure we can work something out."

"Thank you, Bobby," she said as she came again.

After cuming about five or six times she curled up and went to sleep. It was two thirty in the morning when he pulled into Salt Lake City, at the train station.

"Baby wake up and put your panties on. We are in the city and the Mormons, don't like it when girls run around without panties."

After she was all proper and back together, Robert pulled up in front of the station. A red cap came out and began unloading the baggage, then called on his handy talkie,

"Hertz? We have one of your vehicles out in front."

Robert handed the red cap his tickets and a ten-dollar bill. The man told Robert to take the tickets with him and he would take care of the luggage. He then said,

"Mr. And Mrs. English, if you go in the front doors, you will see a large red sign that reads "FIRST CLASS LOUNGE". Go in there and show them your tickets and they will get you anything you require. Just then the Hertz man came out rubbing his eyes. Robert gave him the keys to the car and the paperwork.

"Mr. English, do you want to fill the car with gas, or do you want me to do it and charge it to your card?"

"Thank you. You do it, I'm kind of tired." Robert handed him a five-dollar bill and the Hertz man drove the car away.

Katie and Robert went into the first-class lounge and showed the clerk their reservations. He checked them through and said,

"There are complementary drinks and sandwiches in the refrigerator along with snacks and fruit. There are sleeping seats in the dark area over there. If you wish a nap, I will personally awaken you prior to the arrival of the California Zephyr."

They both picked up a can of juice and lay down in the seats. She looked at Robert with her bottom lip sticking out and said.

"Eighteen hours Bobby?"

Robert just smiled at his little sister-nun-nymphomaniac and said,

"Go to sleep."

What seemed like just a few minutes later, Robert and Katie were awakened by the clerk and told that the train would be there in ten minutes and would layover for thirty minutes before it departs. There was an electric cart to take them to the train. Katie felt like a Queen, as she had never been treated this well before. She was a happy girl. They were at trackside when the train rolled in, and the redcap who had taken their luggage, guided them onto the train and down a narrow hall to their stateroom.

"This is it Mr. and Mrs. English, first class. I believe you and your wife will be very comfortable. The porter will be in just a few minutes to make up the bed." Robert handed him another tip.

"Thank you again Mr. English." With that statement the red cap departed.

"Did he say bed? We have our own bed on the train Bobby?" Katie asked with a broad smile on her face.

Robert just smiled and sat back waiting. She sat on his lap and said,

"Bobby you are just a big tease. I thought we were just going to sit next to ..."

".... each other," he said finishing her sentence. "I know what you thought. For somebody who has been a nun for so long, you show very little faith."

A knock came on the cabin door, and the porter was told to come in. Quickly he set up the bed and put away their clothing. He pointed out the restroom, which included a shower, then after receiving a tip from Robert, he was on his way.

"What do you say Ms. English, would you like to go to bed?"

"Would I? Just let me put on my nighty."

Katie took a green nighty out of her overnight case and went into the bathroom. When she came out, she sat on Robert's lap and began kissing him on the neck, in his ear and all over his face.

"Two days ago, Robert, I only remembered you as a little boy. Now you are the center of my universe. I love you so much, I don't know what to do."

"Get into bed and I'll be right with you."

Robert quickly stripped down to nothing and crawled into bed with Katie. The bed wasn't very large, so they were lying close together. Katie didn't mind a bit, deciding that things would work better if he were behind her. As the train began to move, they opened the window shade a little. It was completely dark outside as Katie reached around behind her and began to stroke Robert's penis.

She lifted her right leg and told him,

'Bobby ... push your cock in me and fuck me a little ... please."

Robert took hold of her hip, moved in closer and slid his cock into her tight little pussy. She groaned as she felt the large member fill her vagina. She was happy every time she could involve Robert in her sexy scenarios and have access to any part of his body.

"Robert ... do you think it would be possible to fuck all the way to San Francisco?"

Robert grasped her hip with his right hand and took hold of her hair with the other. When he shoved his cock into her and pulled her hair, she loved it and came right away. She was so happy they were going to be able to have sex for the next eighteen hours. As Katie had her legs squeezed together, it seemed even tighter than normal. She began working her "kegel" muscles again squeezing his cock.

Robert loved to fuck his sister as much as she wanted him to do it to her. They were the perfect couple. They loved each other because they were brother and sister, but also because they were perfect sex partners. He couldn't believe how good it felt to slide his cock into her gorgeous slippery pussy. The train was moving out of Salt Lake, with a gentle rocking movement that assisted in their lovemaking, and the more he pulled her hair, the more she came.

"Oh, Robert fuck me harder, and pull my hair again. You are such a naughty boy, and I love being naughty with you."

He rolled her over on her stomach, and got on top of her, shoving his cock into her as hard as he could. She was going to say nothing, as she was now his love slave, ready for everything he was going to give her. Accepting everything he offered her.

When he leaned forward, and licked the back of her neck, she couldn't stand it and began to cream all over his cock. Telling her to turn over, she did as he asked and laid herself open to his assault. He jammed his cock into her hard and she hooked her legs around his, so he couldn't get away. As he fucked her harder and faster, she held him close aware her was going to fill her vagina with his fluids.

He was moving fast and had a pained expression on his face. She knew he was ready, and squeezed her titties together, telling him to suck on them. He took a warm soft, yet firm mouthful of her titty, and sucked. She squealed and oozed out a tablespoon full of juice wetting his penis again.

As he was sucking her titties, he felt the most wonderful feeling in his thighs. It was warm, and it tingled; then a slight pain hit the back of his neck. His breathing increased and he could hold off no longer. All of his cum began to shoot out the end of his cock, into his sister's pussy. She took a deep breath, her toes curled down and she grabbed his ass with both hands as she came again.

They lay there as the train moved down the tracks toward San Francisco. The steady rocking of the train was gently putting them to sleep. Robert then realized he was on top of her and moved off, taking her in his arms and holding her tight. She was very comfortable and moved a leg over him. The liquid from her pussy was leaking on his thigh. She kissed him lightly on his lips and said,

"Eighteen hours!" then giggled and drifted off to sleep.

Robert was awakened when the train lurched and made a loud noise. He looked out the window as the sky was beginning to turn from black to a light blue. Watching the passing scenery, he saw the sun come up on a new day, a day that would begin to make his life really worth wile. His older, little sister lay in his arms sleeping, content and happy. He snuggled down into the covers and went to sleep.

A knock came at the door around eight-fifteen. The porter was advising them breakfast was now being served and would continue until nine-thirty. He awakened Katie and whispered in her ear that they should get up for breakfast. She looked at him and smiled then kissed him on the lips. He got up and went into the bathroom to pee. She was right behind him, and then reached around and took hold of his cock.

"What are you doing baby?"

"I wanted to help you Robert, so I thought I could hold it for you while you peed. Girls never get to hold anything when they pee."

Robert thought, 'what the hell; if that's what she wants to do then why not let her.' It felt funny, peeing and not holding on to his cock. She was a good shot, however and aimed right for the pot. When he was done, she shook it and then took a warm washcloth and washed it carefully. After several minutes his penis began to get hard, and she had him sit down on the commode. She then knelt down in front of him and took his cock in her mouth. As she began to suck, Robert wondered at his fortune.

About five minutes of her special nurturing was all he could take and he told her he was about to cum. She nodded her head, which added pleasure to what she was doing. Robert stiffened his back and legs and began squirting his cum in her mouth.

"Mmmmmm," she said and swallowed it, "Now I'm hungry, let's go to breakfast."

As Robert was getting dressed, she came up behind him, put her arms around his neck and bit him on the ear.

"Oww. What was that for?"

"I just want you to know that I love you."

"Don't you have a less violent way of showing me?"

"Sure ... let's go back into the bathroom."

"No let's go to breakfast instead."

"Okay ... your loss."

They locked the stateroom and then he guided her down the narrow hallway toward the dining car. When they got there, they had to wait for several minutes until a table was available. When they finally sat down, he handed her a menu. She said,

"I'll take one of everything. You really know how to stir up my appetite."

Robert began to write the items of food on a menu card for each of them.

"Baby?" he asked, "Do you want eggs?

She nodded her head.

"How do you want them?"

"Scrambled ... light."

"Bacon or sausage? And what kind of toast? Coffee or milk? Orange juice?"

"I'll have whatever you are going to have, Robert."

When they were waiting for the food, Katie reached across the table and took Robert's hands, looking him in the eyes.

"I love you, and I'll do anything for you, no matter what."

"The same goes for me too, Kitten. No matter what."

They ate breakfast and watched the scenery of western Utah, as the train headed for California. She talked about everything that happened to them in the last two days, and suddenly tears began to form in her eyes.

"What's wrong baby?"

"Nothing Bobby. I'm just happy. Happier than I have ever been in my whole life."

"You make me happy also, Kitten."

"Thank you, Robert. I will be thanking you every day for the rest of my life."

"That's not necessary, sweetie. I should be thanking you, because you saved me too."

"From what Robert?"

"Loneliness, boredom, a dull life and about a thousand other things I can't talk about in mixed company."

Katie smiled and her deep dimples excited Robert.

"Could we have a little wine, Robert?"

"Of course. What kind would you like?"

"Something light and fruity, but not too dry ... Okay?"

Robert ordered two bottles of White Zinfandel and took them back to the stateroom. When he closed the door, she took the 'do not disturb' sign and hung it on the doorknob.

Robert opened a bottle and poured them both a glass. They drank a little, and then Robert got down in front of her where she was sitting on the bed and slid the bottom of her skirt up to her tummy, revealing a pair of Raspberry colored panties. He placed his hands on her knees and slowly pushed them apart, moving his head between her thighs, kissing them on the soft inside, just below the crotch of her panties.

As Robert licked her thighs, she moaned and ran her hands through his hair, pulling his face gently into her crotch. When Robert saw the dark Raspberry colored stain on her panties, he leaned forward and kissed it. She groaned and began to play with his ears as he brought her extreme pleasure.

He then took hold of the elastic and pulled her panties to the side, sliding his tongue up and down her slit. She was breathing hard when he took her clitoris between his lips and sucked on it. Two minutes later she began to dribble her juice out onto Robert's tongue.

He grabbed the top of her shiny panties and pulled them down over her hips. She lifted her butt as he pulled. Taking the panties off her legs, he dropped them on the floor and placed his whole mouth over her clitoris and pussy lips. Sucking hard, she came again.

Closing her eyes, she reveled in the feeling of her legs wide open and his head between them, his mouth sucking on all of her tender parts. After she squirted again, Robert stood up and removed all of his clothes, then turned her over on her stomach, shoving one of the pillows under her mid-section.

He moved in behind her and placed his cock at the entrance to her pussy hole, then shoved and pulled on her hips at the same time. He began fucking her as hard as she wanted it and continued on through at least four orgasms. Robert was about to cum when she screamed into a pillow and splattered one more time hard against him.

Not pulling his cock from her pussy, he leaned in top of her, resting on his knees and elbows, moving his hips slightly. She hugged her pillow and moved her hips back into him, her pussy sucking on his deflating penis.

When it came time to have lunch, the porter awaked them. Robert thanked him, however declined stating they were going to catch up on some much-needed sleep. As soon as he was gone, they lay in each other's arms totally naked kissing and touching. They played together all afternoon, and their play culminated in a wild no holds barred act of pure sex, fucking each other as hard and fast as they could.

When the dinner bell rang, they were up, showered dressed and ready. They were both starving. All through dinner, Katie smiled at him, her deep dimples accentuating her natural beauty. Robert was truly in love. They returned to the stateroom, and Katie said,

"Bobby, don't be angry, but I have something I have to tell you."

Fearing the worst Robert asked. "What?"

"Bobby my pussy is a little sore ... maybe we can wait until tomorrow? If you need me, I'll suck you?"

Robert began to laugh and said,

"You know Kitten, I'm a little sore myself. Maybe we should pace ourselves."

They both laughed and he poured out more wine. They held each other then finally laid down for another nap. The train pulled into the "Fisherman's Warf" station about ten thirty at night. As the porter had packed their clothing, and taken it off the train, Robert and Katie, got off. After eighteen hours on the train the aroma of the San Francisco bay, was a wonderful change. Katie had never seen an ocean in her entire life. The red cap, at Robert's request, hailed a taxi for them.

Robert helped her into the back seat while he assisted the driver with their baggage. Robert said,

"Mark Hopkins please."

"Yes sir."

"Where is the Mark Hopkins, Robert?"

"You will see little one."

Katie looked like someone who was watching a tennis match. She was trying to look in every direction at the same time and see everything.

It only took about ten minutes from the Warf to the top of the hill, where the hotel is located. As the taxi pulled into the circle driveway, a valet opened the door. Robert paid the taxi driver and slipped a bellman five dollar to get their bags. At the front desk, Robert signed the register as Mr. and Mrs. Robert English.

Katie was delirious and wasn't sure what would be next. As they went up the elevator to the ninth floor and the honeymoon suite, he told her they would be staying in San Francisco for three days, and the following day he was going to take her to Ghirardelli Square on a shopping tour, then lunch at Alioto's Restaurant on Fisherman's Warf, and later to Chinatown for dinner, if she wanted.

In the suite, they stood by the window and looked at the sights of the city by the Bay and contemplated their new life together.

If you would like this story, then please leave a review on amazon it really helps.

If you love this story, then please find more books from Tandem House Publishing. Don't worry Richard has more books on the way.

MILE HIGH MICHAEL: AN EXHIBITIONIST'S ADVENTURES IN JAPAN
BY: RICHARD PUMP

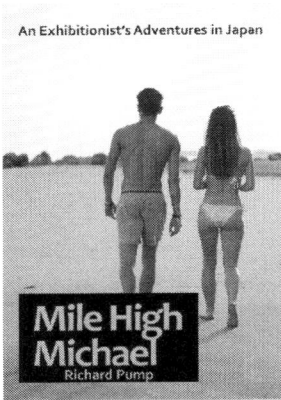

An Exhibitionist's Adventures in Japan

Mile High Michael
Richard Pump

One Man's Journey to have the hottest experiences of his life.....

It started as a chance meeting in an airplane. Neither of them knew that their love would bloom into something that would change their lives forever. A desire that can only be quenched by meeting someone that you connect with in a completely new way. After a plane ride, Michael would never be the same. His love life and his knowledge of Japan will have ever changed. A desiring heart knows what it wants, and sometimes you can find it a mile high..

BAD TEACHER: A STORY OF A MOTHER WANTING MORE

BY: GEORGE PUNWELL

It started as a forbidden love. A mother's desire to make love with her son's teacher, and for her to be left breathless and satiated by another woman. A love and satisfaction that can only be brought on by someone with so much in common. After an evening of passion, Kelly and Stephanie would never be the same. Stephanie would never be able to love David in the same way again. A heart knows what it wants, and sometimes that love is forbidden.

A Nun's Tale

SWINGING A CRAZY GAME OF POKER

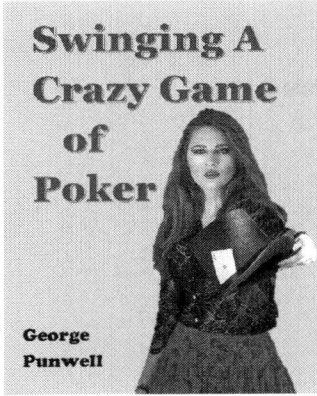

BY: GEORGE PUNWELL

Bob's wife Sandy had been interested in expanding our sex life to include other people for some time. Bob had been flirting with Linda, a married woman who worked with me for several months. Soon a game of poker was going to change all of their lives.

WHAT TO EXPECT: A short story, with erotic love stories between groups of consenting adults. MFF, MMF, FF, MF.

Printed in Great Britain
by Amazon